The Promised Princess

Lashell Rain

This novel is a work of fiction.

All characters and events portrayed are products of the author's imagination and are used fictitiously.

Sir Gavin was used with the original cosplayers permission.

How the author portrayed the character was a complete product of the author's imagination.

Dear Reader,

This book contains mature material

material includes:

Battle Scenes, Blood, PTSD, Physical & Emotional Abuse, Mature Sexual Content, Violence & Death

Cover designed by MiblArt

Contents

To Dawson: Thank you,
your creativity is inspiring.

Follow Dawson,
the cosplayer of Sir Gavin here:

www.tiktok.com/@dawson_mullins1

Chapter One

MYLA

Scrambling, I shoved the leftover loaves of bread and cheeses from tonight's dinner into a makeshift bindle from my bedsheet. A family in Baela spoke to Harper about their needs while she was at the market earlier today. I hadn't planned on sneaking out tonight, but I couldn't stand by and do nothing. I had been sneaking food and medicine out to those that were poverty stricken for so long that they knew if they were in need to find Harper at the market.

Over the last few days, I had been asking for extra food at mealtimes: apples, grapes, anything extra to help. I was sure the cooks thought my appetite grew more and more every week since more families had been coming to me for help during their times of distress. The guards would start their shift changes soon, and that was the only time I could sneak out of my room without being noticed.

Everyone was so used to seeing their beloved princess dressed in the kingdom's finest attire with a crown upon her head. They would never suspect a thing when I snuck out in between shifts wearing the leathers of a female guard. I felt more myself in those clothes than I did in the royal ones.

I cracked the door to see if the coast was clear before throwing the hood of my cloak up over my head, opening and shutting the door lightly behind me. I walked nonchalantly down the marbled hall to the winding staircase of my tower. Throwing the bindle over my shoulder, I felt the fruits tumbling around in there. I hoped no one took notice of my makeshift bag. If someone saw me, they were going to think I was stealing from the Princess instead of being a guard that protected her.

This was the most food I had ever tried to sneak out with. Harper had told me it was a larger family needing my help. I rolled my eyes at the thought running through my mind of what I must look like to the outside world. A hushed laugh escaped my lips as I approached the stairs. I quickly descended them, doing my best to breathe naturally like I did this all the time. I didn't know how the guards walked this whole castle all day long while doing rounds. This was my home and I could barely make it down a spiral of stairs without needing to gasp for air.

When I reached the bottom, I let out another huff, trying to get my breathing to return to normal. The small hall that opened up to the sitting foyer had double doors leading to the gardens. I glanced around to check for knights again before the beautiful scent of wildflowers seeped into my lungs as I took in a drag of the fresh air. I looked back for a moment before I rushed down the narrow paths, hugging the edges of the garden and out towards the giant metal gate.

Slipping between two broken bars hidden behind a tree, I looked over my shoulder again to be sure no one had followed me before I pulled the food through the hole. I had known about this part of the gate being broken for weeks, maybe even months now, and I knew if I let my father know, he would have my head for keeping it from him and using it to sneak out at night to take a walk. Alone. Which was something I never got to do.

Anywhere I went, a guard or escort accompanied me. They were always three paces in front of me or behind me. Royals were not supposed to associate with any of the lowly people, but I viewed them all as people just the same. To my father, the idea of taking a walk alone would be absurd. That was how all of this began: a walk. And then, upon seeing the conditions of my people, I had to do something, anything, to help.

Was it considered stealing if it was my food to begin with? To me, it wasn't, but to my father? That was an entirely different story. I walked a few more paces before getting behind one of the larger trees and bringing the bedsheet down to the ground and letting it go. I scurried back to put some space between me and the care package. None of the families knew who left the food. I assumed they thought it was Harper, but I didn't know for sure. I watched a shadowed figure approaching through the trees, and as they came into view, I noticed it was only a child. Normally, I let them take the food and leave, but this wasn't normal.

"What's your name?" I whispered from the shadows.

"Agnes," her small voice called to me. She couldn't be over eight years old.

"Where are your parents?"

"They are too sick to get out of bed." Her statement made my heart clench. "I hope this helps, Agnes. I'll try to get medicine next time."

"What's your name?" she asked, and I could tell her childlike curiosity was getting the best of her. I hesitated for a moment, but I told her anyway. Maybe it would give her hope that not all royals were the same.

"I'm Myla," I whispered back, and I heard her gasp in surprise.

"Myla... the Princess?" she spoke almost to herself, and I could hear the disbelief in her tone even though I could barely see her features through the darkened woods.

"Yes, the Princess, but let's keep that our little secret, okay?"

"Okay," she said as I heard the crunch of a guard's boots bringing me back to the situation at hand. I was the Princess of Baela, outside the castle walls, past the gates, with no one's knowledge. Now I had to sneak back in and pray to the gods that I didn't get caught. I never had, but I didn't want tonight to be the night that I did, over the only way I knew how to help my townspeople. I glanced around the tree I was tucked behind before preparing myself to run back to the double doors, into the foyer, and then up the stairs again.

"Go Agnes, hurry, get out of here!" I said as she grabbed the makeshift bag, but as she pulled it up and over her shoulder, fruits started falling out. I shoveled them back in quickly, tying the sheet tighter.

"Go!" I said while pushing her off, and she disappeared into the night. The thought of her family brought a small frown to my face. I wished I could do more, but if any knights were close by, I couldn't take any chances. Looking around the wooded area one last time before hurrying toward the broken metal gate, I heard the sounds of a guard's footsteps approaching again, making me crouch back behind the trees.

I tried to remain still and as quiet as possible. My heartbeat thrummed in my chest at the thought of being seen. I looked around the tree, not seeing anyone, and made a run for it, but I didn't make it over three steps before a muscled arm pushed out in front of me from the other side of the tree and clotheslined me to the ground.

My breath left my body as my head ached from slamming into the hard soil. I looked up to my attacker. The dark spots cleared from my vision as he glared down at me; his smoldering stare quickly turned into a surprised expression. His wide blue eyes met mine, and I realized he had seen my face.

"You're the Princess. I—Your Highness, my apologies." He reached down to help me up, pulling me back to my feet like my weight was nothing. Looking me up and down for any further injuries, he noticed the leathers I was wearing.

"You okay?" he asked, and for the first time, I got a good look at the most attractive man I had ever seen in my life. He looked away for a moment, checking our surroundings, and I caught myself roaming over his body before he looked back at me again. His jawline was strong, filled in with groomed stubble that wrapped from ear to ear. His hair was longer on top and trimmed up on the sides. I looked up at his eyes, watching the moonlight dance in them, and I realized I had been gawking at him in silence this whole time. He probably thought that he had broken me or something.

"Your Highness." He moved closer toward me, his brow furrowed, but he stopped himself from getting too close. "Why are you outside the royal gates in the middle of the night?" He looked concerned.

"It's a long story." I looked away, feeling the flush creep over my cheeks

"I'm sure you can tell me all about it on the way back up to your room." He spoke with a sweet, amusing tone to his voice as his worried expression faded.

"You have a powerful right hook," I said, and my blush turned into burning hot embarrassment. I wanted to lie back down on the ground and bury myself under the soil at how absurd I sounded telling this man how strong he was after he took me down. He let out a laugh at my comment, looking back down at me again as if he were trying to find an injury. He stood almost a foot taller than me, and even though he was wearing armor, he didn't have his helmet on, showing me his light brown hair. The emblem of two swords was etched on his right shoulder plate, the emblem of my kingdom, although it had never really felt like mine, more like I was just a pawn in my father's game.

"I'm okay," I reassured him, and he glanced away.

"What are you wearing?" He looked puzzled, like he was trying to place all the pieces together.

"The guards' leathers? What do you mean?"

"Those haven't been worn by the guards in months. Do you sneak out often? If so, we need to strengthen the security around here if the Princess can just sneak out in the middle of the night in old leathers."

I scoffed. "Maybe I'm just that stealthy."

"Ah." He smiled again. "I'm sure you are many things, Princess, but stealthy is not on that list." I rolled my eyes at his response.

"Well, it's worked for this long," I reminded him.

"Why are you out here again?"

"Uh—a rat got loose in my room and I was trying to set him free." At this point, he couldn't tell if I was telling the truth, lying, or trying to end our ridiculous conversation.

"It looks like lying isn't a strong feature of yours, either. The Princess of Baela sneaks out in the middle of the night alone to set a rodent free, risking her safety in the process by slipping through the royal gates?" He paused, looking back down to the ground where a single apple was lying close to where I stood and picked it up. "With apples?"

"Myla," I tried to change the subject.

"What?"

"My name is Myla, and technically, I'm not alone anymore. I'm with you. What's your name?"

"Gavin, Sir Gavin Dawson, pleased to make your acquaintance, Princess, but we really need to get you back inside so I can report to the King—"

"Don't!..." I cut him off before he could finish his statement. "Please don't tell the King I was out here." He glanced back into my eyes for a moment as if I were asking him to sacrifice his honor to our kingdom by withholding information from my father.

"Alright..." He hesitated before continuing. "...but you need to get back to your room. I'll escort you, but I will tell your father about the hole in the gate afterward."

"That's fine. Just don't tell him about me."

"Deal." He held out his arm in front of himself, urging me to walk in front of him to escort me back to my room, but I stood and walked next to him.

"I'm fine right here, thank you," I said, and he gave me a surprised expression before I looped my arm with his, following the direction of where his arm was pointing. The cool metal of his armor seeped through the sleeve of my leathers, making me shiver and stand a little straighter. I had never been this close to one of my escorts before, except for Harper. Especially not walking back to my room, but we were alone, and I didn't want to be like all the other royals who thought too highly of themselves. We walked in silence for a long time, making our way back through the garden. I paid attention to the flowers of all shades of color, trying not to look at him until he finally spoke.

"Was he a big one?" he asked.

"What are you talking about?" I furrowed my brow at his question.

"The rodent? Where I'm from, they're massive. I'm surprised a lady like yourself wrestled one out of her room," he joked. Gavin knew the rodent story was complete rubbish, but it warmed my heart that he was going along with it, anyway.

I snorted out a laugh and instantly felt the heat rush to my face again. I couldn't remember the last time I had an informal conversation with someone who genuinely wanted to talk to me. The only people I ever had any interactions with were those snobby wives of my father's councilors because those men refused to talk to a woman, even if she was a royal princess. They had looked down their noses at me my entire life. It had never bothered me. I had never felt like I belonged here anyway. I was at my happiest outside the royal gates on those few occasions I had snuck out, whether it was for a walk or some of my other shenanigans. Eventually, I had to tell Harper about my little late night adventures. That was around the time we started helping the townspeople with common needs. She was really the only person who had ever treated me like a normal human being with feelings rather than an object. She had definitely covered for me multiple times in the past. I looked up at Gavin this time before going wide-eyed with excitement.

"He was massive. I didn't think my sheet was going to be big enough."

"A sheet?" His smile reached his eyes again as we made it to the top of the stairs.

"You caught a field rat in a bedsheet? Now I'm even more impressed. You're definitely not what I was expecting, Princess."

I didn't know why, but watching him pause and turn toward me with that ridiculous smolder sent flutters to my stomach and into my chest. Before I noticed, I looked to the right and realized we were already standing in front of my room.

"And what exactly were you expecting of your princess, Sir Gavin?" I said, turning to him.

"I don't know, but it definitely wasn't you chasing rats in the middle of the night. Most women around here wouldn't even want to go outside because the wind would ruin their hair." He played charades, acting like one of the royal castle women, and I let out another laugh. He opened the door for me, and I let go of his arm, and for a moment, a tinge of sadness passed through me. This man had been kind and one of the few people other than Harper to be genuine, and the idea of watching him leave, having the conversation end, made a frown tug at my lips.

"Have a goodnight, Your Highness." He nodded.

"Just Myla is fine."

"Myla," he breathed it softly, almost to himself, as if savoring my name on his lips, before looking at me one last time with those sea-blue eyes. I had never been to the sea, but I had read stories about how beautiful it was, and I imagined his eyes would be the same color as the ocean at sunrise. He gave me one last nod of his head before I walked into my room and shut the door behind me.

Gathering my thoughts on everything that had happened, my anxiety got the best of me. What if he told my father that I was out there? If he told him about the gate being broken, I wouldn't have a way to sneak out anymore. The walls in my room, as big as it was, felt like they were caving in around me as I thought about never being able to leave this place other than for mealtimes and a garden walk if I was lucky. Should I tell Harper about this knight? Maybe I shouldn't because she could be a little overdramatic about men. I began stripping off the leathers and walked into my closet, which was filled with my royal dresses and nightgowns.

Throwing the dirty leathers behind me into the hamper, I settled on a navy-blue gown that matched the royal color of my kingdom. It used to be gray, but I guessed my father decided he wanted to add some color to it. I slipped it on over my head, and the smooth, cool silk felt comfortable against my tired muscles.

After running around for the last couple of hours, I must have done more than usual, which normally wasn't much, being a sheltered princess. Or maybe it was because I got pummeled to the ground by a charming knight in shining armor. No, it couldn't possibly be that. My lips curled into a smile.

I really should start trying to learn more to protect myself. Hopefully, Harper brought the dagger I asked her for. I was so sick of feeling defenseless and weak. I did not know how to wield a blade, but I was sure it wouldn't be too hard to learn, and with all my free time in my room, I was positive I could learn. How hard could it be?

Getting on my bed, I scooted myself up to lean my back against the golden, upholstered headboard, grabbing my off-white covers and pulling them up over me. The chill of the night's air crept through the thin nightgown I wore. I looked around my room and wondered what it would be like to be free. Free of the kingdom's duties as a king's royal object. My father ruled the kingdom all on his own and never included me in anything. I never got the chance to grow up with my mother. She passed away from a deadly sickness when I was young, or at least that was what I was told.

I remembered her walking me through the gardens all the time, and then it was like she vanished overnight. A few days later, my father told me she had passed, and I remembered crying at the loss of her, but I was so young. It was a distant memory now. I cherished the small memories I still had of her. Sometimes I wondered if my upbringing would have been different if she hadn't died.

My father had been absent from my life, mostly. Ever since my mother died, he had relied on the servants of the castle to raise me. The only time he wasn't absent was if he brought forth a punishment. It didn't happen very often since I did well to keep my little ventures a secret and cover my tracks. Maybe that was why my brain couldn't turn these racing thoughts off. Tonight was the first night somebody had ever seen me after I left my room, other than Harper.

I guessed all I could do now was hope that Sir Gavin Dawson was a man of his word. The thought of him brought a small blush to my cheeks. He was the first man I had ever talked to that wasn't in his late fifties staring down at me from his high horse at a councilor meeting or at the royal dinners in the castle. The first male that I had ever had a decent conversation with since I couldn't remember when. Sure, I had shared a few improper endeavors with male servants before, but not very often. Now that I thought about it, I couldn't remember the name of the last servant I had an encounter with. It had been a while.

Anytime guards escorted me somewhere in the castle, they rarely spoke to me. One walked a few feet in front of me, and the other walked a few feet behind me. Harper always walked next to me and told me about the castle gossip or about her friends in the servant quarters on the other side of the castle, which I had never been to or seen.

My father had always said that the servants were too lowly to talk to, but from my experience, they were more kindhearted than any of the royals I had met over the years. Although Harper and I didn't see eye to eye all the time, I still considered her my best friend, but she could be a little much with her vivacious personality. She was definitely loud and could be a little obnoxious sometimes, but she had a pure heart and meant well.

I pulled myself from my thoughts and lay down, tucking myself deeper between my covers, trying to get comfortable and calm my anxieties, as if that were possible. Tomorrow morning Harper would be here to wake me up and help me get ready for the day as I put on my fake royal smile and mannerisms and laced up my corset like the good little princess I was. If it were my choice, I'd be a simple town maiden with a small but quaint home and a loving husband and maybe even have a small family one day. But I was stuck in the tower of my own royal castle as a prisoner princess, daydreaming about a simpler life.

I felt myself doze off, away from my thoughts. I sank into my bed as my body loosened up from the stress of the day. A knock at my door brought me back to consciousness. I rose from my bed, mind groggy. The light wasn't shining in from my balcony like it did every morning. It was still the wee hours of the night. I glanced back through the glass, balcony French doors at the horizon, seeing the faint glimpse of pink rising from above the ground. Who could be up at this hour?

I grabbed a robe and walked myself to the door, but before I got the chance to open it, it flew open and almost knocked me out. Harper came barreling in, wide awake, as if it were time for lunch. I watched her wiping the sleep from my eyes as she started ranting about some male servant she had been interested in recently, but I barely caught anything other than they touched.

"Harper, wait. Slow down. What?" I gently shut the door behind her.

"We touched Myla! We were both heading to the dining hall at the same time and he told me he thought I looked lovely when we passed by each other. Later on, he grazed my hand and gave it a squeeze as he passed! Myla, I think I'm in love! He's so dreamy! And—"

"Harper. Hold on. You've only been talking to this guy for a few weeks. Don't jump the wagon for him just yet."

"Oh! Pish posh! It's love! We are meeting for lunch in the gardens, and I'm so excited, Myla!"

I wanted to share the excitement with my friend, but being a princess who was looking in from the outside of every situation, I had seen this happen more than once over the years. I had watched female and male servants "date," if you could even call it that. The men these days took advantage of the female servants' feelings until they got what they wanted, which was usually sex, and then they would leave the woman heartbroken. I didn't want that to happen to Harper.

"Could you say something!? Instead of just giving me that blank stare!" Harper's squealing brought me back to reality, and, although I wanted to tell her exactly what I was thinking, I responded the best I could.

"Be careful. Some men can be cruel sometimes and I don't want you getting hurt."

"Really, Myla?" She rolled her eyes and flopped down on my big reading chair in the corner. "Can't you be happy for me, just this once?"

"I am happy for you. I wish you well on your date." I faked a smile.

"Gosh, sometimes I think you're the one who needs a man in your life. You're so cynical all the time."

I changed the subject as she pulled her feet up onto the chair and wrapped her arms around her knees, "on the bright side, I snuck out some food for that family that came to you from the market."

"How are they? They seemed so desperate for help. I had to tell you about them." Her voice was soft.

"I don't know how the parents are; their daughter picked up the package"

"Well, did you make it back in time before the knight's shift change?" She flipped her short red waves over her shoulder as she looked over at me. I hesitated to tell her about Gavin, but I had held nothing back from Harper before, so I told her anyway.

"I got caught."

"You what?!" She jerked her head up with fear-filled eyes.

"But—I met a knight, and he escorted me back to my room," I said while looking out of my balcony doors. The sunrise was in full bloom now. The warm glow of it seeped into my room.

"A knight! Myla! Why didn't you start with that? You almost gave me a heart attack thinking you got caught sneaking around." A smile curled up on her face before she continued giving me a naughty side-eye. "Tell me about him!" Her voice echoed off the gold and white decorative walls of my room.

"Shhh. Could you keep your voice down? Goodness! Remember, nobody knows I sneak out. Don't be announcing it to the world."

She got closer to me, grabbed my shoulders, and pulled me in. Her bright red lips were only a few inches from my face.

"Tell me everything!" She squealed in a hushed tone this time.

Harper was definitely overdramatic, but I told her everything about what happened with Sir Gavin Dawson and how he made me feel.

Chapter Two

GAVIN

I walked back to my guard post smiling to myself and could not get Myla's image out of my head. A royal princess in guard leathers sneaking out in the middle of the night did not scream royal to me at all. Her reasoning was pitiful but I played along. When I was around her, I didn't feel tense and wound up as I did with most royals. Actually, that was how I felt most of the time, not just with royals.

She seemed so free-spirited and her smile... God, not just her smile, all of her was ravishing. Her black hair made her sky-blue eyes shine through the night, and her lips when she would flash that pouty smile toward me filled me with warmth. I thought I was going to fall over at her beauty.

No, snap out of it Gavin. What the hell was wrong with me? I just met her and my mind was already racing about being around her.

No, that wasn't possible. I was just a gate knight of the royal palace from a small town in Baela. I was not royalty or rich. The Princess would never be with a man like me. Being the eldest sibling from my house, they drafted me for war the moment I turned eighteen. I had seen death in more ways over the years than most. That I was sure she had never seen. I would want no one to see the things I had. The thoughts I had of her a moment ago, I believed, were the most absurd thoughts to have ever crossed my mind. A royal princess would never want to be with a man as damaged and as lowly as I.

I got back to my post right before the morning shift change, thankfully. I couldn't imagine what the punishment would be for leaving your post. This job was important to me. It paid well, and my mother needed the extra money I sent her to keep the farm running back home. But I couldn't let the Princess of Baela walk back to her rooms alone in the middle of the night. Though if anyone asked, I wouldn't be able to tell them. She asked me not to report seeing her outside to the King. Which would mean I couldn't tell any fellow knights either.

Why? I did not know. I could only assume even the royals got punished for actions they knew they weren't supposed to do. All I knew was that when we went through training as a knight, we were told the Princess was never to leave the royal castle. I couldn't blame her for wanting to sneak out. If I were stuck in my house all the time, I would get stir crazy too. Though, she lived in a castle, and it wasn't like it was a small home or anything.

Roland's heavy hand coming down on my shoulder jolted me out of my thoughts, and I realized just how distracted I had been since getting back to my post, thinking about the Princess. I instantly straightened myself, trying to look more focused than I was.

"It's shift change. Go get some sleep, Dawson." He addressed me by my last name just like we did when we used to fight together in the war. Roland was the only brother-in-arms I had left that was in the same battalion as me. We were both drafted at eighteen from the same small town when the war started six years ago. When it ended, we were both sent here as knights to the Royal Castle of Baela to serve as protection for the royal family.

"See you at the mess hall," I said before walking toward the front gate entrance to the castle to give my overnight report to the equerry. Roland gave me a cocked smile and a simple salute with his fingers before he turned away to make his rounds. It didn't take long to get to the equerry office. I walked up the stone steps to get to the grand entrance of the castle. The two knights on duty tipped their heads to me in greetings and let me pass. I walked into the small office to the left of the main entrance where Fredrick was waiting for my report.

"Oh, hello, Gabe." He waved his hand toward me dismissively, busying himself with the scattered papers on his desk before asking, "Anything new to report?" He didn't bother showing respect to anyone he believed was lower than he was, knights included.

"It's Gavin, sir," I said sternly, trying to hold back my tongue at his impertinent tone. "And—" I stopped myself. I didn't know why the Princess was sneaking around last night, or why my conscience was telling me not to report not only her whereabouts but also the hole in the gate, but I didn't. "No, nothing to report, sir."

"Thank you for your services, Gabe. You're dismissed." He didn't notice my pause and continued his reading. It took everything in me not to knock his snarky, imperious tone right out of his mouth. He looked up and gave me another small wave of his hand as if telling me I could see myself out, and I left without another word because if I spoke anymore to this man, I was going to kill him for his lack of respect and arrogant attitude.

This was how we knights were used to being treated, or really anyone who wasn't from a family with money. The royals believed they were better than everyone else only because they were born into a royal bloodline or were full of wealth. This was why I was so taken aback by meeting the Princess and having her talk to me as if I were in the same social class as her. After making my report, I realized how tired I was from walking the grounds all night. I made my way back to the knight's quarters on the outskirts of the royal grounds, which were nothing special. Every knight got his own bed, a side table, and a small locker for what few possessions we could fit in them. I kept two sets of clothes in mine and some things that reminded me of home.

My armor and weapons stayed under my bed, close to me in case of an emergency. I quickly changed, trying my best to be quiet as the other men in the large open quarters were sleeping. Getting into bed, the exhaustion of the night before slowly took over, and I quickly fell asleep with the Princess tucked away in my mind. No nightmares came for me.

Chapter Three

MYLA

Harper had been rambling about what was trending around the kingdom markets. With clothes, jewelry, and makeup, the woman always strived to look her absolute best. It was something I had always admired about her. She was beautiful with her sun-kissed skin, short but full soft red curls, bright red lips, and piercing green eyes. No wonder when we walked together she got more looks than I did. I had never cared much for appearances. After being showered with wealth all your life, you grew to love the simpler things.

I had never been that good with makeup, either. Harper taught me how to put on what little I used now. Having servants always painting my face with it got old. I wanted to have independence—control over the smaller things in my life. My appearance was one of them, although my father disapproved. A little kohl liner and that was usually it for me, other than when Harper would beg me to let her do it.

My skin had always been lighter. I blamed my father for my complexion, considering I was only allowed to go outside for a short walk in the garden around mealtimes, and then it was back into the castle. That was where Harper and I had just come from. Servants could not sit with royals during meal times. So we grabbed something small and ate out in the gardens together before heading back to my room.

"What do you think?" Her question caught me off guard as she flipped through the ring of color swatches in her hands. I knew nothing about fashion, but I knew that she always looked amazing in red, so I went with that one.

"The red one," I replied quickly, assuming she was asking my opinion on her dress color for the ball happening within the next couple of weeks. If I had the choice to not go, I wouldn't. It had never been fun for me to dress up and play nice with all the royals. The only reason I would go was because Harper wanted me to, and I couldn't deny that I usually had a good time with her. Plus, the wine was always worth it.

"Were you even listening to me?" She looked at me with a side-eye.

"Harp, you know I know nothing about fashion or makeup or any of those things. But I do know you look amazing in red." I winked at her

"I do, don't I!" She flipped her hair and gave me a devilish smirk, and I laughed at her facial expression. The sound of clicking heels and chatter below made me crane my head over the edge of my balcony. Harper followed suit. The wives of some of my father's servants were passing below. One had stopped in the middle of their chatter to ask the other to tighten her corset, causing her voluptuous curves to bust even further out of her already tight dress. They spoke to each other without a care in the world.

"Did you hear King Ferand won't be coming to the ball?" The woman tightening the corset spoke, while the plumper woman held her breath through every tug. Her face looked like she was changing colors from how tight the other was making it.

"I really need to ease off the cheese," the plumper woman spat, and Harper and I tried to hold back our snickers. They both shot their heads up toward the balcony from the sound. Harper and I fell to the ground before they could see us as they went back to their conversation.

"I heard Ferand isn't coming because he's quite ill, but his son responded to the invitation. He will be there, Tilly, that boy you always drooled over at the parties." The plump woman laughed.

"I did not!" But you could see her cheeks redden even from up here as we glanced back over. "And I think you need to hold off on more than just the cheese, Darla! Goodness!" Tilly tugged one last time, almost as if she wanted to punish Darla for the embarrassment of her childhood crush.

"Just tie my corset, Tilly! And be polite or I'll snap you like a twig," Darla spoke to Tilly as she finished tying the corset and started straightening her dress.

"Maybe you'll get your chance. I hear he's looking to court."

"I will look my absolute best for the ball," Tilly spoke with a confident smile as Darla offered Tilly an arm and they continued their walk to wherever they were headed. Harper and I gathered back in our seats, composing ourselves after hearing the royal chatter.

"Well, it looks like you have some competition from Tilly on the Prince of Credia," Harper said as she twirled a finger in her loose curls, teasing me.

"She can have him. I think I'm the only woman who doesn't fall to her knees and swoon for him."

"I believe that's why he has always been so fixated on you, even before the war started. Does he still send you love letters?" She asked, grimacing at the question.

"You're probably right, and no, not since the war ended."

"Did you keep the old ones?" she asked, and I rolled my eyes at her.

"I used them for kindling, remember?" She let out a loud laugh. The memory of us sneaking into the wine cellar and stealing the fanciest bottle of wine we could find while staying up reading the letters and tossing them into the fireplace afterward crossed my mind. Apparently, it had slipped from Harper's, but we had far too much to drink that night.

From a young age, my father used to have parties and balls all the time, and the Prince of Credia was always there trying to get my attention, even though he had the eyes of every female our age. It was almost like it wounded his ego that I had never been interested in him. His need for attention and his brazen attitude reminded me too much of Fredrick, my father's closest advisor.

Once the war started, the get-togethers stopped, and he started sending letters expressing his so-called affections. I sent him one back politely, explaining my disinterest, but he sent more anyway. Harper and I used to read them like dirty jokes until they stopped when the war was over.

I didn't look forward to his presence at the ball if he really was going to be there. I looked off to the right of the gardens to the sound of metal on metal clanking in the distant field. The knights were training with their swords in the open, and I couldn't help but wish there was a way that I could learn how to fight and defend myself too.

A glimpse of light-brown hair caught my line of sight, and I followed it to that familiar face. The knight that clotheslined me to the ground and then escorted me to my room with kind eyes and conversation was sparring with another. I smiled to myself at how outrageous our first meeting was. Harper must have noticed because when I looked back at her, she was giving me wide eyes and grinning like a schoolgirl at me.

"What?"

"You like him!"

"Harp, shhh, the entire kingdom will hear you." I turned my head to glance at the knights to be sure nobody was hearing our conversation before I went on, as if they could hear us from this distance.

"That's absurd! I could never be with him. My father would never allow something like that."

"Oh, my gosh! You're not denying it!" She squealed in a hushed tone, trying to contain her excitement at me showing interest in something she had an interest in: men. "We only just met, Harp. It isn't like that." She ignored me.

"Which one is he?" She pointed toward the two men that I was looking at. Both were shirtless and you could see the shimmer of sweat covering their muscular bodies from the heat of the evening sun. I pushed her pointed finger down immediately, feeling the blush rush to my cheeks.

"Harp! Quit being a devil-may-care and mind your business!" I said swiftly, giving her a prudish glare before glancing back at the knights again.

"But if you must know—" I smiled at her. "—he's the one with the lighter hair." She squealed with excitement for me again while grabbing both of my hands. For a moment, I felt like she was going to jump up and down, so I was glad I had a hold of her. We looked back over at the men training again and watched them as they moved so effortlessly with their blades. Almost like a war dance around one another. Out of the two knights fighting, one had black, shoulder-length, braided hair with deep caramel-toned skin, while the other was a man I had come to recognize: Sir Gavin Dawson.

They both must have felt our eyes burning holes through their bodies because they both looked up at my balcony at the same time, and Harper and I quickly looked away, acting as if the dress colors that Harper was still holding were the most interesting thing we had ever seen in our lives. I didn't know what made us both look up again a few moments later, but when we did, they were both looking at us with smirks on their faces. As if saying "we caught you" with the looks they gave us.

I waved at Gavin and he waved back, giving me a wink, and for a moment, I giggled to myself with Harper, a heavy blush taking over my face. I gave him one last look before we both stood up and went inside, cackling together. I realized I had needed it. I had not had a good laugh in a long while.

I helped Harper tidy up my room, made my bed, and organized my clothes. Sometimes I would forget that she was my royal servant. I told her all the time that I would do everything, and most of the time, I would. Or we would do it together to save time so we could have tea on the balcony, or she could tell me about what it was like outside the castle gates. I'd always dreamed of just walking through the kingdom during the day. Things that were probably simple to most would be so much fun for me: shopping for clothes or picking up my food, talking to the townspeople about their problems.

I had always said that if I ever were to become queen, I would want to make a difference in the world, but other times, I felt my father had already done too much damage. King Henry, or shall I say, my so-called father, was the one who caused the war against the other two kingdoms over something as trivial as territory. He sent his knights to the borders for selfish reasons. I had never understood how the loss of lives was worth the extra land. My father had always been power hungry. If it were up to him, he would expand the Kingdom of Baela and get rid of the others.

None of the kingdoms had ever gotten along, really. Baela was the biggest and wealthiest of the three from the livestock commerce. The outskirts of Baela were full of farmlands for the trades, feeding the mouths of those who could afford it, of course. How else had my father become the wealthiest?

The Kingdom of Credia and The Kingdom of Mayri were the other two. Both were sister kingdoms. They used to get along with one another. But the King of Credia, Ferand, had a falling out with the Queen of Mayri. They used to trade different textiles and fine silks. I wasn't sure what happened between them. My father only allowed me to know what he felt was enough, but if Credia was no longer trading with Mayri, I didn't know how the Queen could afford the financial burden of her kingdom without trade.

The Kingdom of Mayri was the second biggest of all of us. Their queen, Lilith, had been ruling her kingdom as a young widow. Her husband died some years ago, shortly after they married, but she continued to rule alone.

I was worried about how the ball would go because it was only a couple of weeks away. The rulers had not been in the same room with each other in over a year, since they stopped all the fighting and bloodshed. The Kings and Queen were supposed to be there, but Ferand never responded to the invitation based on the royal chatter I heard with Harper on the balcony earlier. Instead, his son would be there, and even though Ferand was just as vile as any other royal I had met, I preferred the father over the son. He was the eldest of all the rulers, so I could only assume he fell ill because of his age.

I helped Harper gather up any leftover soiled laundry and walked her to the door, preparing myself to walk down to the washroom with her just as an excuse to leave my room with her as my escort, but she had other plans.

"I'm meeting Tomas in the washroom. Maybe you could come with me next week." She spoke quickly, like she was in a hurry to do my laundry, and I realized I had forgotten to ask what the man's name was that she had been so infatuated with lately until I heard her say it.

"I thought you said you guys weren't seeing each other until lunch?" I questioned.

"We are still having lunch, but he wanted to see me sooner, so this was the only time we could meet." She spoke with a wide smile, but a part of me felt like she was hiding something from me. I didn't push any further. I just rolled my eyes.

"Fine, have fun," I said with a wave of my hand.

Hearing the door shut, I walked over to my bed and threw myself back on it with a huff, wishing I had something to do. The thought of Harper going to see Tomas made the image of Gavin come back to mind. I imagined him during his training, how he swung the blade so efficiently, never missing his mark. I could tell that it was something he had grown comfortable with—fighting in the midst of battle. A part of me felt sad at the thought of him only knowing war and bloodshed for all those years. The things he must have endured during the war. I was sure that was why he took his duty as a knight to serve and protect the royals so earnestly.

I had a deep respect for this man, and yet, I still barely knew anything about him other than he had a strong right arm. I smiled to myself, getting off the bed, and walked back to the French balcony doors to look out the window to see if I could catch a glimpse of him again. Turning my head to look at the open field the knights were training in, my sights snagged on something red. My eyes went wide, and my mouth parted.

It was Harper. In the gardens. With Gavin.

I fell back against the wall and felt the heat rush to my face. My heart pounded in my chest. What was she doing? What was she saying to him? I leaned over to glance back out the window again and this time they were both looking up at me, and I felt like I was going to faint from embarrassment. It took everything in me not to march down there and drag her back up to my room. You know what? I would. I was going to do it.

I ran to my bedroom door and swung it open, hastily moving one foot in front of the other through the hall, down the stairwell, and through the garden doors. Hearing the doors swing open, Harper turned quickly. She eyed me with a smile on her face. I darted out toward her in a brisk walk, trying my best not to look embarrassingly red at the thought of what she could have possibly been saying to Gavin. I approached them, and before I could say anything, Harper spoke.

"Gavin said he would love to escort Your Highness to the ball if you'll have him." She gave me a devilish grin at what she knew she had just gotten away with and then gave me a small bow of her head before prancing off back to the door. Harper picked up the laundry she had left sitting there on the ground. She wasn't meeting Tomas. She glanced back at me, proud of what she had done.

"Devil-may-care," I mumbled under my breath toward her as I watched her saunter off.

"Ahem." Gavin cleared his throat, and I turned to him.

"I'm sorry, she's a bit mad," I said, trying to calm my nerves as he let out a small laugh.

"Well, if you truly want a knight to escort you to the ball, I'm yours."

I'm yours. His words sent a shiver down my spine.

"I'd love that," I replied, trying to hide the nerves in my voice. He gave me that side smile, the same side smile I had been seeing in my head since the last time I saw him. I fully took him in. He wasn't wearing his normal attire of armor, just a white tunic with the buttons undone revealing his bare, muscled chest with brown trousers. His hair was still tousled from sweat from the knight's training session. I looked away, letting my mind linger too long on the sultry thoughts I had about this man. I tried to hide the heat rising within me again. Why did he make me feel like this just from a smile? And then it hit me.

Sir Gavin Dawson would escort me to the ball. Was this a date? I knew he would only be my knight escort, and that was not really considered a date. But despite that, he would be there instead of guarding the gate for the night. We would both be at the ball. Together. I looked back up at him for a moment, and he held out his arm to escort me back to my room.

Oh, my gosh. My room. I left my room. I had been out here in the open with Gavin. Alone, with no escort. No permission. Outside the castle walls. He must have seen the panic on my face because he didn't stop himself from asking.

"Myla, what's wrong?"

"I—" But before I could finish, one of my father's royal assistants, Fredrick, came from behind me, and I felt his tight grip on my forearm. His fingers dug in, making his hold painful.

"Your Highness, your father would like a word," he hissed in my ear. Gavin must have seen the terror building in my eyes because he put his hand on Fredrick's arm and pulled me from his hold.

"I'll escort her," Gavin seethed.

"I beg your pardon. You're off duty, Gabe. Go back to your quarters," Fredrick spat back.

"On or off duty, she is still my princess to protect."

My princess. Gods, this man was going to be the death of me.

"Well, you can protect her when you're on duty."

"It's okay. I'll be fine. I'll see you soon," I spoke up, taking Gavin's hand in mine for a moment, and I tried to sound reassuring, but after seeing my reaction that I desperately tried to hide when my father wanted to have a word, I didn't think he believed me. Gavin gave me a nod of his head.

"My lady," he muttered before turning to leave. He gave Fredrick a look filled with venom.

"If you'd like, Gabe—" Fredrick exaggerated the name, knowing it was wrong. "—you can escort the Princess back to her rooms after she speaks with His Majesty." He spoke to Gavin in a condescending tone while showing him a wicked grin at the end of his statement.

“I’ll be there,” he said through gritted teeth as his jaw ticked from Fredrick’s insolence.

Before I had the chance to object, Fredrick pulled me along to the King’s chancery. I glanced over my shoulder and watched Gavin's long strides toward the knight’s quarters. A part of me hoped he wouldn’t show up to escort me back to my room. Not because I didn’t want to see him, but because of what he would see when he got there.

Chapter Four

MYLA

Fredrick and I walked down the long stone hall that I had been down so many times, and it led to those dark wooden doors. My father's office. The quiet stretched down the arched walkway. I paid attention to the sounds of my footsteps ricocheting off the walls through the silence. Looking at the insignificant details of the paintings that lined the walls, I tried to keep my mind distracted from what was awaiting me. The tall windows let the light from the sun brighten the hall that normally looked grey, and it filled my heart with indignation.

Fredrick paused in front of the door for a moment as if he took pleasure in my dread before lightly knocking. Hearing the door creak open made my heart clench in my chest. A woman sauntered out, dressed as one of my father's harlots. She looked down at me like I was less than the dirt under her threaded gold heels. Only the best for one of my father's whores.

Her dress, if you could even consider it clothing, brushed against me as she stepped out, hitting me with one of her shoulders before letting us pass through. The sheer black fabric clung to her breasts and barely covered anything with the long slits that went to both of her hips. The gold jewelry around her neck, wrists, and in her ears covered more skin. She turned and gave my father a small bow of her head. I got a good look at her before she walked away. She had an odd familiarity to her before she shut the door behind me. Hearing the thud of the heavy door closing made the office feel like a cage closing in around me.

On either wall were bookshelves up to the ceilings, with old tomes and novelties. My father never bothered to read. My mother was the one who loved reading, and seeing him turn this room, her favorite room, into his own torture chamber spat on her loving memory.

There was a long moment of silence while my father finished his liquor and poured another for himself. Looking over the rim of his glass, he stood, taking down his second drink in one swig before he strolled around his large desk that sat against the back wall of the room. He set the glass down with enough force his gold rings clanked loudly against it. As he turned to face me, I jumped from the sound.

"Oh, Myla," he said under his breath, "I thought you had enough of this? But I guess you never learn."

"Father plea—" Before I could finish, I felt the searing heat of the slap across my face as it jerked my head to the side from the impact.

"Shut up," King Henry whispered to me. He was so close I could smell the lingering liquor on his breath. It made my skin crawl. I looked straight at him, cooling my features. I would not let him get the pleasure of seeing my pain—my fear. He lunged for me again and I couldn't stop the small flinch from happening. My body reacted on its own. He smiled to himself before looking over at Fredrick, who was beaming about the show he was getting to watch.

"What should we do this time, Fredrick?" He looked at his royal advisor. His friend. The man who had watched every punishment given to me through the years. Or given them. "I believe I got to have all the fun last time, so would you like a try?" My father asked while he gave his friend a heavy hand on the shoulder, pointing to the smoothed, polished desk where a small whip lay across it. It was one of the many tools of his punishments. I closed my eyes for a moment, trying to collect myself and catch my breath before they continued. My father addressing me brought my eyes back to him.

"Strip, Myla." I didn't argue. It was pointless to try and stop the inevitable. I undid my corset, letting it slide to the ground, before I took the straps of my dress and pulled them down over my shoulders, my clothes fell to the floor. The cool air sent a chill over my bare back.

"Now sit," he demanded.

Henry grabbed a small stool for me to sit on from the side of the room and I complied. I readied myself for what usually happened next. I'd spent too many days with my naked body lying against the chilled floor, finding some reprieve against the burning pain of his lashings. I looked forward and followed my father's movements as I recalled my past inflictions.

He ran his ringed fingers through his slicked black hair, his eyes so dark they almost looked black in the dim lighting of his office. Fredrick was holding the whip in his hand as he walked from my father's desk to stand next to me. Sitting on the small stool made them both tower above me. My father gave the nod, and Fredrick raised his arm above his head and brought the whip down with full force over the tops of my thighs.

I gripped my fingers around the round top of the stool as the searing pain rushed through my body. I prepared for the agony of the next strike. My breath hitched as I tried to breathe through it.

"Do you know why you are being punished, Myla darling?" My father's voice called from behind me as he put his large hands down on my shoulders and rubbed them mockingly. The anticipation of the next blow was another method to his torment, as he always enjoyed dragging out the punishment.

“Because I left the castle without permission.”

“Exactly,” he said as he leaned down to whisper in my ear, taking my hair and twirling it around one of his fingers. "And what happens when you don’t listen to your father?”

“I get punished,” I said, trying to keep my voice from breaking.

“Correct again.” He stepped back and Fredrick brought down three more blows over my thighs. I could feel my blood glide down my legs. The tears built behind my eyes from the pain. I held back a sob as my body trembled. My father wiped some of my blood onto his fingers.

“Tsk.” He sneered, shoving it into my face, pressing his fingers against my already bruising cheek. “Look what you made me do, darling.”

My tears fell, and there was nothing I could do to hold them back any longer. Fredrick brought down the whip. Again, and again, and again.

My father pulled the stool out from under me and I fell to the ground. My legs were nothing more than bloody welts and cuts from the leather. The pain was so great that they were almost numb. How I found the strength to stand, I did not know. It must have been the adrenaline making my legs hold my weight. I wiped away the last of my tears, smearing blood across my cheek as my father walked back to his desk. He poured two glasses of amber liquid this time, while Fredrick walked to the door, cracking it, and mumbled to someone.

Henry pulled open a drawer from behind his desk, wiping his bloodied hands clean with a rag before grabbing his golden crown and placing it back upon his head. He stood tall and walked the drink over to me.

"Take it. You need it more than I." But I didn't take it. The disgusting things I felt about this man outweighed everything else. The pain, the punishments, the rules. I gathered the spit in my mouth and sent it flying into his face. I knew it would just cause me more treachery, but I didn't care. My father took the liquor, throwing it down over my legs. The burn made me scream as I stumbled to the floor. My breath labored, and my legs convulsed from the sting.

My father looked down at me with snake eyes as he pulled his hand back to slap me again. I fell flat against the ground, my body lurching from the impact.

"Get up. Get dressed. And get out."

I found my dress close to me on the ground and threw it on quickly. Fredrick grabbed me by the crook of my arm and dragged me to the door. I tried to gather my footing but my legs failed me. Upon opening it, he threw me out, and I landed on a hard chest plate. Warm hands grabbed me and held up my weight, keeping my legs from giving out.

Sir Gavin Dawson was most definitely a man of his word. I looked up at him, and the anguish of what was happening washed over me. I didn't want him to see me like this.

Broken. Frail.

Weak.

And bleeding, after my father and his disgusting royal councilman whipped me until I cried out from the pain. I looked away from his eyes as they looked over me, assessing the damage. I didn't know what I looked like, but when I glanced back up at him, his expression told me I must have looked as bad as the pain soaring through my body felt. His deep blue eyes were mixed with hatred and compassion. For a moment we were both silent, but the thud of my father's office door closing brought us out of our trance and back to reality.

"Myla... If I would—"

"No, don't do that. It's not your fault. It's nobody's fault but my own." I spoke with ragged breaths, trying to get enough air into my lungs. Pushing myself out of his arms, I tried to move, stumbling down the long hall to get back to my room. I'd crawl if I had to; it wouldn't have been the first time. I tried to keep my legs steady but failed miserably, almost falling back to the ground. Gavin caught me again and hauled me up in his arms. As my long dress draped over my thighs, the blood from my wounds seeped through my gown.

"Shit, Myla." His voice was low and hollow. Gavin noticed the blood, and I couldn't hide the shame I felt from him seeing me like this. Having to carry me to my room, bloodied and beaten. I knew Fredrick had done this on purpose when he told Gavin he could escort me afterward. It was all for a power play against Gavin, knowing that he wouldn't be able to stop what happened, knowing it would bring me shame having Gavin see me like this.

I could feel the tears welling up in my eyes again, and I looked away from him, trying to hide the emotion in my voice as I spoke.

"Please, just get me to my room, and get Harper; she knows what to do." My voice broke, and Gavin just held me tighter in his arms as if knowing that I didn't need his words, only his silent comfort. He made haste toward my room, up the spiraling stairs. The movement made me feel dizzy as the adrenaline subsided and my mind felt groggy from the pain. I leaned my head against Gavin's chest, hoping he didn't think differently of me now. The prisoner princess of her own castle. A weak, spineless woman.

We approached my door, and I lifted my head and went to stand, but he didn't put me down. He nodded toward the door handle and I opened it as he carried me into my room and took me straight to the bathing chamber. He sat me down in the tub, turning the golden knobs that released warm water from the faucet.

"What are you doing?" I asked, glancing up at him as he grabbed a few rags from the cupboard before walking back toward me.

"I'm not waiting for your friend. I want to help, if you'll let me." He gestured to my gown as a request, and I accepted his offer. I slipped the gown over my head with a wince so I didn't have to move my legs and tossed it onto the floor, hearing it splat against the marble. I looked away anxiously as he used lavender soap and warm water to cleanse my wounds. Once he got to some of the more sensitive ones, I gripped the edge of the tub from the pain.

"I'm sorry," he mumbled but stayed focused on my thighs. He grabbed another rag and placed it in the warm water and moved to my face. He lightly dabbed around my bruised cheek and nose. I pulled back a little from the ache. When he moved away, I could see the blood on the rag and realized my father must have done more damage from his last blow than I originally thought. I was so caught up that I didn't notice until now. His eyes met mine, and I couldn't hold back the tears that slipped down my cheeks.

"Hey." He placed a gentle hand on my cheek.

"I didn't want you to see me like this: beaten and bloody. You probably view me differently now."

"If anybody knows anything about being beaten and bloody, it's your knight, Princess." He gave me a small side smile, and I reveled in it. His smile brought a jolt of joy through me like I'd never felt before. It made me forget about the pain, if only for a moment. The pull I had toward this man, I couldn't describe. But I never wanted it to go away.

"How do you think I see you?" He furrowed his brow at that, and his attention was fully on me now that my injuries had been cleaned. I crossed my arms over my chest to cover myself.

Humiliation blanketed me, but there wasn't much I could do about being completely bare in front of him.

"Someone who's weak." I looked away, but he gently placed my cheek into the palm of his hand again and pulled my eyes back to his.

"You are the furthest thing from weak, Princess," he assured me. His eyes held mine before he lifted me out of the water, helping me to my feet as he unplugged the tub. He grabbed a towel from the counter and bent down in front of me and started drying my ankles before working his way up my calves. I looked straight ahead as the heat rushed to my face. The warmth spread to my core as he worked his way gently past my wounds and then to my lower back. He stood, and the intensity of his stare overpowered everything else until it was only us in the room. The pain, the anxiety, the disbelief of my feelings faded, and it was just him. We could see each other in the same light. As two people who knew what it was like to be beaten, bloodied, and alone. I looked away, and he backed out of the room. He came back a few moments later with a nightgown and left it on the long counter.

"I'll let you get changed," he said soothingly before he turned to leave the room, shutting the door to the chamber behind him. I let out a deep breath before finally looking at myself in the mirror. I could only imagine how horrible my wounds were before the bath, as my mouth gaped at how terrible I appeared. My cheek had already turned a deep purple that would soon fade to green and then back to my normal light skin. The blue eyes staring back at me, which were normally bright, looked more gray and puffy from crying. My dark hair was a mess, but I didn't care.

I let the towel fall away to the floor and picked up my bloodied clothes from the ground and tossed them in the waste bin. It was something I had always done. I never wanted to be reminded of the beatings, so I would throw the clothes away afterward. Carefully, I put the new gown on and slowly brought it down over my mangled thighs, trying to hold back the tears again at how badly they hurt. I opened the door and leaned against the frame to hold up my weight on weak legs. I thought Gavin had already left, but he rushed to my side and gathered me up into his arms again, walking me over to my bed.

My arms naturally wrapped around his neck, and I looked up at him as his scent engulfed me. He smelled like a midsummer night, as if the surrounding air suddenly filled with the smell of rain and sweet woods. My eyes fell to his lips and then back into the deep abyss of his stare. As I took in his faint scent, he looked me over. His lips were so close, we were sharing the same breath. Before I lost my courage, I leaned forward and felt the warmth of his lips against mine.

For a moment, he didn't kiss me back, but then he pulled me deeper into our kiss, laying me down on the bed. His hand slid up my back, getting lost in my long hair as he grabbed at the nape of my neck. I tilted my head to give us both more access to each other. My heart smashed against my ribs, and I felt the heat roll through me in waves.

But as quick as it was there, it left. The softness of his lips, his breath, was gone. He pulled back, pressing his forehead against mine with his eyes closed. I feared if he pierced me with his stare, I wouldn't be able to stop myself from feeling the warmth of him again, his lips, his hands. I placed my palm against his cheek and he gently kissed the inside of my hand before he placed his hand over mine. He opened his eyes, looking at me for the first time since our kiss ended.

"Ahem." The sound came from the door. We both looked wide-eyed toward the door and Harper was standing there with a basket of bandages and an assortment of medical ointments. "I heard from some other servants that you were being escorted to your room from the King's office, so I rushed here. But if this is what it's like to be escorted by a knight to your rooms, then where is mine?" She gave us a flirty smile, and I bit my lip, trying to hold back the grin. Gavin got to his feet and took a few steps toward the door.

"I must go, Your Highness." His voice was gruff and breathless. He looked at me one last time, his eyes filled with a mixture of emotions, but the one that was most plain to me was sorrow. But behind that, I could see the desire in them. The thought almost took my breath away. My knight and I. Together. I didn't know what it was like to be involved seriously with a man, and until a few moments ago, I didn't know that you could have a kiss as passionate and needy as ours was.

My body didn't want him to stop. I wanted him to keep kissing me, and if Harper wouldn't have come in, who knows how much further we would have gone? I felt this push and pull with Gavin that I had never felt for anybody. Is this what the start of love felt like? I barely knew the man, but the thought of not seeing him from on my balcony or at the royal gates when I snuck out at night made my chest ache. Gavin walked past Harper and out of the door before anyone could say anything further.

Harper's face practically glowed with excitement as she rolled up and down on her heels, gracefully coming over to the bed, but that was when she noticed the damage done. Her face fell from the happiness she had before, and she started doctoring my wounds, taking the cold ointment and gently dabbing it on before she wrapped my upper thighs with the bandages she brought with her. She had done this so many times she knew how to do it without causing me too much pain. Harper had been my royal servant for years now. She had seen every punishment. Some were worse than others, but every time, she was always there to help me. Once she was done, she turned to me, beaming again.

"How was it?!" Her voice was filled with excitement. She obviously didn't want to talk about the dreadful punishment by my father; she wanted to focus on more joyful things.

"I never knew that a kiss could feel like that," I said while dragging my fingers softly over my puffy lips, trying to remember what Gavin felt like against them. What he tasted like.

"See! I knew you liked each other." But the smile tugging at my lips quickly faded at the reality of our situation. I was a trapped princess by my father, the King of Baela. Gavin was a lowly knight. We were from two completely different worlds. And the world that we were living in would never allow us to be together, no matter how much we felt about each other. If he even felt the same as I did.

Chapter Five

GAVIN

What am I doing? Why does she do this to me? I barely know anything about her, but everything in me burns for her. I watched her stumble out of those chamber doors as that prick of an equerry, Fredrick, just tossed her around like she was garbage. I almost lost it until I saw how hurt she was, and then my only focus was getting her to her room to help her. Seeing the blood soak through her gown made me absolutely hate myself for pledging any type of loyalty to a king that would treat his own daughter this way.

I didn't think. I just acted. I put her in the tub, asked for her permission as she lay bare to me, and washed off the blood and filth from that room. She didn't want to look at me. Didn't want me to see her cry or show me how often this had happened throughout her life, but while I was tending to her, I saw the leftover scars from the past. It made me want to slay the King and all of those who fell loyally behind his disgusting behavior.

She hid it too well. Princess Myla always graced the royal grounds with a smile on her face. She seemed adventurous and kind and everything I would want in my life. Something I needed more of in my life. Ever since the war ended, I had been so lost, so broken after all the bloodshed, all the hatred. But when I was around her, it was as if I had been found. The cloudiness fell away and everything in my mind shifted to her.

She kissed me, and I couldn't stop myself from kissing her back. Her soft, pouty lips covered mine. I devoured every inch of her mouth and I didn't want to stop myself. I hoped she didn't think that was all I would want from her. She wasn't someone I'd want only for a night.

When I was in the barracks and trenches of war, anytime the knights could get pleasure from the nurses on sight, they would. I had a few during my time there, but most of the time I would resort to my hand. My mother raised me to respect a woman's choices, and that was what I always tried to do. But with Myla, I wouldn't just want her for a night. I'd want to see her bright blue eyes look at me every morning.

I had to stop this. We couldn't continue whatever this was between us. I was not royalty. She needed a war-torn knight for her protection, and that I was. I wasn't here to be loved or favored by Her Highness. I was here to serve, and that was it, and it needed to stay that way. The thought of me and Princess Myla being together was impossible. Even if she felt the same.

Lost in thought, I made it back to my post. The light was fading over the horizon, and I needed to start my rounds. Quickly I walked, feeling as though I were in a race with the sun as the sky was changing from blue to a dusky sable. I looked up at the pale crescent in the sky and I couldn't help but think of Myla.

I knew she must be in pain from what happened today. The long welts over her thighs looked like some wild animal had clawed her. As I was thinking about it, I figured out why he did it to her legs. With her being the Princess of Baela, no one would ever see her thighs unless they saw her in a nightgown. He had been hiding his abuse from their kingdom. How many people knew the true colors of the evil king they stood behind?

They led me to believe that King Henry was a respectable man who lost his wife and was left to raise his daughter alone. Did his wife die from a terrible sickness, as everyone thought? Or did he beat her to death when she disobeyed? Like he beat Myla when she did something as simple as leaving the castle. That man sickened every nerve in my body. My fists clenched at my sides at the thought of him laying another hand on her. Making it to my post at the gate, I saw Roland standing there and my brow furrowed.

"What are you doing here? I thought you worked the day shift?"

"Yeah, I was on day shift until today. They rotated the knights again," Roland responded, and I cursed under my breath.

Every few months they rotated us; we changed from the day shift, to the night shift, to the tower. Which meant I was supposed to be walking the tower—Myla's tower. I ran a hand down my face at possibly seeing her so soon after our heated encounter. Roland just looked over at me and smiled.

"You've got it bad for her, huh?" He said it while crunching down on an apple he must have grabbed from the dining hall, when he was getting his schedule change. He grabbed his skin of water, bringing it to his lips.

"Yeah... I kissed her." I said it almost as if I were still in disbelief about it myself. Roland spewed his water, getting choked up on bits and pieces of his food, and I couldn't help but laugh at his reaction to my sudden confession to a fellow man-in-arms and a friend. Roland and I went way back, so I felt comfortable enough to tell him, but nobody else needed to know.

I was lowly, and knights shouldn't even be touching the royals. We were here to protect at a distance. That was why, when the Princess got escorted, the knight stood a few paces in front or behind her. The thought of me walking next to Myla the night I caught her sneaking around snagged my mind. She never tried to correct it, never tried to push me away or act as if she were better than me because of her social class. My chest ached at the thought of me carrying her up the round stairwell while trying to get her back to her room. She was completely and emotionally broken after what her father had done to her. How he allowed her to be treated by Fredrick. The anger rose in me again, but Roland, coughing on any leftovers in his mouth, made it hard to be angry.

"You did what?!" He wiped his mouth and looked up at me.

"I kissed her, and I think I'm growing feelings for her,"

"Oh Gavin, you know better, mate. You need to end this fixation with the Princess. It'll cause you more trouble than good." He clapped his hand down on my forearm before pulling me into a one-handed, quick hug. He let go and pointed to the tower. "You better get going. Now would be the perfect time to stomp the flame." I gave him a nod of thanks for the advice before treading my way back to the Princess's tower.

I went through the garden and came to the double doors to the foyer, beyond it was the twisted stairwell leading to Princess Myla, which was how my stomach felt. Twisted and in knots at the thought of losing something that wasn't mine to begin with. I walked the stairs, feeling my chest tighten with every step closer to her.

When I reached the top of the stairs, I stopped and looked down the hall toward her room. Instead of walking over there and knocking to tell her we had to stop all of this, I simply walked the other way. The hall wrapped around the tower where the Princess stayed. Both sides led to a dead end as her room sat in the center of the tower.

I paced the hall from one side to the other all night, trying to tell myself to knock and end this before it went any further, but I couldn't. Every time I wrapped back around to her room, I paused a moment in contemplation. Not in regard to ending it all, but I was trying to hold myself back from opening her door to check in on her. Trying to gather enough self-control to stop the want that I had to wrap my arms around her again and tell her she was safe. By the time the sun rose in the east, I realized that these feelings that I had for Myla were just as strong as the rays clinging to the earth at dawn.

I made my way back to the garden foyer, cursing myself for not being brave enough to confront whatever this was that was happening between us. Walking out toward the dining hall, I saw the same redhead who asked if I would escort Myla to the ball. I believed she said her name was Harper. She was quite rambunctious compared to Myla, but she seemed kind. I could tell Myla and her were close because anytime I saw one, I usually saw the other. She walked toward me, and before she got the chance, I blurted out what had been on my mind all night.

"How is she?" Harper gave me a light smile before speaking.

"She was doing fine when I left her last night." She spoke to me in a hushed tone, taking a few steps back a moment as she quieted her voice while some of the King's royal servants passed by with their haughty stares filled with disdain. It made me want to knock their teeth down their throats.

At that moment, something occurred to me. Did all the King's royal servants know what he inflicted on his own daughter? Most of the time, the royals didn't even acknowledge my presence, but Fredrick had seen me and Myla interacting in the garden and he had come for her.

I was sure some servants saw me carry Myla to her room because I felt as though there were a lot of eyes on me. I shifted on my feet at the unwanted attention. Harper nudged me along to walk with her toward the dining hall as she kept speaking.

"But that's not why I came to find you. In two days, there will be a royal dinner to finish up the last bit of planning for the ball. Since you're the tower knight, you'll be escorting Myla and me there."

I took a deep breath; I knew I wouldn't be able to walk the halls and avoid seeing her forever, but I had at least thought I'd get more than a couple of days to mull over my thoughts about what to do or say to her. I couldn't just walk up to her and tell her I had feelings for her. I'd look like a fool for just thinking about us being together. It was almost as if Harper could sense where my mind was going based on my face alone.

"If you're worried about Myla liking you or not, I can affirm that she most certainly does." She tossed her head over her shoulder to look back at me as we approached the dining hall doors.

"It's not about us liking each other; it's about the fact that being together is forbidden. It's impossible."

"So you like her too!" She squealed way too loud considering we were at the doors of the mess hall filled with people on the other side.

"Keep it down." I gave her a glare in warning, but it didn't seem to faze her excitement for the thought of two people liking, possibly even falling for each other, and for a moment, I enjoyed it. I indulged in the idea of Myla and me caring for one another with Harper. It sat there comfortably in the forefront of my mind for a moment before Harper spoke again.

"Anyhow, I must go. I'll be heading to Myla's room to check in on her for you." She gave me a wink, teasing me before she walked back through the narrow paths of the gardens. I straightened my back and stepped into the mess hall. The smell of smoked breakfast sausage and the slight sweetness of bread filled my lungs, making me realize just how hungry and exhausted I truly was. I was ready to eat and get some sleep after raking my mind all night about the emotional turmoil happening to me.

The clanking sound of metal on metal surrounded me as the blade of my enemy hissed by my face. I brought my sword down upon the man in front of me and kept moving forward through the fog, shadowing the battlefield like a cloth covering our dead, with Roland watching my back. I lost my father amid the grueling battle.

I searched the dirt-smeared faces of all the knights anytime I could stop to catch my breath. Which wasn't often, and there weren't many of us left. My boots sank into the mud and bloodied fallen knights of war as I trekked on, looking for my father. Before the battle, they assigned us into groups. Roland and I were the only ones left that were a part of our battalion, and my father, if he was still breathing. Roland had his back to mine, fighting through the foes of war. I could taste the salt and iron running down my face from the sweat and blood, but I knew I couldn't stop.

I would not stop.

My father rasped my name a short distance away, catching my attention, and I ran to him. Ran through the few remaining battles between comrades and rivals to get to him. I fell to my knees before him and tried to lift him, but he was hurt. Badly. The meat of his leg was hanging from his muscle, while his blood was flowing like a river. I thought quickly and ripped the loose tunic off of the dead knight out of the many lying on the body-littered expanse around us and wrapped his leg as best I could.

"Gavin... it's too late for me, son," he spoke gruffly.

"No." I used the force of all my weight to stop the bleeding, but my hands were covered in crimson, my fingers sliding over the blood and

sweat-soaked skin. My whole body trembled. I shook my head. "You're going to be fine... Everything's fine."

"I love you, son." His voice trembled. "Tell your mother I—"

"No! You will not die here! You can tell her yourself."

"Gavin behind you—" He yelled, yanking my shoulders.

My father grabbed me, throwing me to the side right before a blade plunged through his chest. He saved me. But all I saw was red. My heartbeat thrummed behind my eyes, and I heard nothing around me. Felt nothing.

I tackled the man that killed my father and ripped off his helmet. My vision tunneled on him as I wrapped my fingers around his neck, his dark brown eyes wide as I felt his airways collapsing while I squeezed, pushing down on him until I heard the snap of his neck. I watched his eyes glaze over in death as they stared out at nothing.

I crawled to my father and lay there defeated—lost. Warm tears streamed down my dirty face, as I looked over at his lifeless body. He saved me and I couldn't help him. The pain in my chest swelled.

"Shit." I heard Roland's voice.

"Gavin, listen to me, you're hurt. I'm going to get you out of here..."

"Gavin... Gavin... Gavin." I felt Roland's heavy hands on my shoulders, shaking me as I came to, gasping for breath, my body covered in cold sweats from the nightmares of war. A few other guards in the room looked over at us but resumed their regular routines quickly.

"Nightmares?" Roland asked, almost to himself.

"Yeah." My voice was raw, as if I had been yelling.

"It's time for our rounds." He stood, already wearing his armor for our shift. "We need to go out for drinks soon." He clasped his hand on my shoulder, giving it a light squeeze before walking towards the door.

Roland didn't ask for information or if I was okay, and I knew why: because we had all suffered from the darkness of the same war.

Chapter Six

MYLA

I had been locked away in my room for almost two days. Ever since Gavin brought me to my room from my father's office, it was like I had been stuck in a mental haze filled with him. All the thoughts that had been running through my mind were about him. I wanted to see him, spend time with him, and get to know more about him.

The thought of his lips pressed against mine had definitely been the biggest recurring image in my mind. I ran my fingers across my lips at the thought. Picturing the kiss that happened on the very bed I was sitting on made my heart jerk. I had never let anyone truly see how broken I was. I didn't think I had even let Harper in that close after one of my father's punishments.

With Gavin, it was different. I didn't want him to leave, and him showing me that kind of kindness and patience had me in utter disbelief. Was this what it was like to be cared for, to feel important? I knew Harper had always been there, and she loved me in a way I assumed siblings would care for each other, but this felt raw and passionate. I was worried that it had been too long since I had snuck away and seen him.

Almost like he might disappear if I didn't see him soon, to assure myself he was here. But I had been focusing on getting the strength back in my legs again. Harper had been staying with me throughout the day and bringing me food and fresh bandages when I needed them. My wounds were scabbed over now, and healing. I was walking again. Every step ached, but it was progress. Bending down, on the other hand, was still too difficult. Almost on cue, my door opened and Harper rushed in with a wicker basket that sent a nutty, garlic fragrance through the room. It smelled delicious.

"I brought the cure to all of life's problems," she said while doing a small little dance in place before walking over to me with her face beaming.

"What is it?" I asked, brow raised. I let out a bemused laugh at her happy dance.

"I brought..." She held out a moment for the suspense. "Trenchers!" She sat the basket next to me as she pushed me over to sit on the bed, getting under the covers too, and then grabbed for the basket to pull out the food. She handed me a giant bread bowl filled with pasta. It had a creamy cheese sauce loaded with butter and garlic. I could feel my mouth watering before I even got the chance to taste it. The smell alone made my stomach grumble. Not waiting a moment longer, I shoved a heaping pile of bread and pasta into my mouth, and I couldn't stop the hum I let escape at how amazing it tasted. The rich cheesy garlic sauce fooled me into thinking that this truly was the cure for life's problems. I looked over at Harper with my mouth full, waving my hand in the air enthusiastically before pointing down to the bowl and rolling my eyes, expressing how delicious these trenchers actually were.

"See, definitely better than any man." She gave me a playful wink as she stuffed her mouth full of more food, and I let out a snorting laugh at her comment, making me choke on a noodle. I thought it was going to come out of my nose. I looked over to see Harper hunched over herself, cackling at me so hard she could barely breathe.

We ate the rest of our trenchers together, not speaking much about anything important until she mentioned Gavin, and I started fiddling with the blanket between my fingers at the thought of them talking to each other again.

"So, I ran into Sir Gavin outside the dining hall."

"Oh no, Harp, what did you do now?" I let out a breath, narrowing my eyes on her.

"Nothing! I just told him he'll be escorting us to dinner since he's the tower knight now."

"The what?!"

"Yeah, he's been walking the tower since—you know." She glanced down toward my legs, but I caught what she was referring to even before she looked. "He's the tower knight for now." A soft smile played on my face, and Harper definitely took notice. Gavin was the only man to see me bare and exposed, not just physically but emotionally, and he had wanted me. Or at least, I believed he did. That kiss definitely made me feel wanted.

I thought I may be falling for him. Was that even possible? I barely knew the man. My smile wavered as I shook my head in disbelief. I had never viewed myself with very high importance. My whole life my father had belittled and beaten me down, and I had tried my best to put on a brave face for Harper and for all the other servants that knew me over the years. But around Gavin, it was different. I didn't pretend or hide. The moment I looked into his eyes the day of my punishment, he saw me, all of me. And instead of looking down upon me, he embraced me and all of my broken pieces.

I realized the reason he understood me at that moment was because I saw it in his eyes, too. He had been through a similar experience with the darkness that swirled through this world. They probably forced him to fight in my father's autocratic war. The only thing that man sought was power, and he would do whatever he needed to get it. He wanted to rule everything and anything he walked upon, and it sickened me that he used knights like Gavin to accomplish his selfish goals. Harper rushed out of my closet with dresses in her hands. I was so lost in thought I didn't even see her get off the bed.

"Now that we've eaten something way better than that so-called father of yours could ever serve, let's get ready! Which one?" She held up two dresses, trying to contain her excitement at one of her favorite things: dressing me up.

Option one was an off-the-shoulder, dark-burgundy long dress that hugged my waist before it flared out under the waistline. The other was a classic baby blue with a short, puffed sleeve. It was more simple, with a square scoop neck, a fitted bodice, and a smaller flare than the other choice. I decided on that one, so I nodded toward the blue one and Harper rolled her eyes at me.

"What?"

"You never pick the one I want you to!"

I laughed at her response and said, "Okay, fine. For the ball, you can put me in whatever dress you want. I'll even let you do my makeup." She gave me a confident, cocky smile that made me almost regret telling her that. She took a deep, gratifying sigh, almost like she was savoring the moment before she looked up to the sky, thanking whatever gods there were before leaping onto the giant bed with joy. After her dramatic display of satisfaction, she got up quickly and pulled me out of bed with her to the bathing chambers to get ready for dinner.

She brushed and pulled my black waves half up, away from my face, leaving them to fall down my back. I put on what little makeup I knew how to, doing my best to cover the fading bruises on my face, before placing my crown on my head. I grabbed a simple pair of flats from the closet. Harper put on the burgundy dress she had originally wanted me to wear. We had always been around the same size, but she looked much more stunning in my dresses than I did. She frequently told me how beautiful I looked, but to me, I didn't compare to her.

Her red hair had tighter curls than mine and was shorter as it hugged her shoulders. She had the left side pinned behind her ear while letting her bangs on the right fall to the side of her face. My dress hugged all of her curves in all the right places. I almost forget to blink, staring at how amazing she looked. She looked more like royalty than I did. She was meant for this life, without the grueling punishments that came with it, of course.

Throwing on a pair of black heels to complete her look made her just a little taller than I was. I never understood how anyone could wear those things, especially walking around the kingdom's castle. I'd die after just one set of stairs from either the pain in my feet or from falling down them. She gave me a quick nod as we walked toward the door to head down to the royal dining room, and I took a deep breath at the thought of having to sit at the table with all my fathers councilors and royal servants as they spoke about their boring lives filled with disdain for all other people of any class other than their own.

The thought alone made me tired, and I hadn't even made it down there yet. Harper opened the door and the man that had come to constantly be in my mind's eye was standing there, looking straight at me, almost like he didn't even notice Harper at the door. He was wearing lighter armor than the last time I saw him, more like guard leathers, but it was a royal dinner, after all. I was sure the full plate, when worn all the time, got heavy.

Harper looked over her shoulder, giving me a flirty smile, and then nodded back to Gavin standing a few paces away in the hall. I smiled at her before turning my head back to him. He ran his hand through his hair, and the tension in the air was so thick Harper and I could make more trenchers out of it. Harper cleared her throat as she walked in between the both of us and walked ahead, leaving us alone behind her.

Gavin stayed far enough away to not look suspicious in the public halls of the castle, but close enough that I felt he could hear my heartbeat pounding in my chest. Over the walk, I caved and looked over to him, and he at me.

We exchanged looks and smiles to the dining hall until we got to the door, and then it was time to put on my mask of royalty. I relaxed my face, raised my eyebrows, and looked as if I were completely uninterested in whatever was happening around me. Gavin brushed his hand along the small of my back, sending tingles licking up my spine, and he moved three paces behind me, which is where my escort would normally stand, before Harper opened the door.

I pushed down the flutters in my stomach and the grin curving up on my lips as we moved forward. We walked in gracefully, shoulders back, heads high. We entered the grand dining space, and the room went quiet. The far wall had tall arched windows opening up to the castle grounds, with intricate designs lined with gold covering the vaulted ceilings, similar to my room. The drapes were the Kingdom of Baela's royal color, along with all the other drapes in the castle. Harper pulled out my chair at the long, sleek wooden table before she pulled out her own as she sat down next to me. My father looked at us with a sly grin on his face, and I swore all of his features darkened as we sat.

"You look ravishing, Harper." He looked at me. "Darling, you should really take some pointers from your servant," he said, glancing between the both of us. His eyes filled with scrutiny as he looked on from the end of the table. His tunic was well embellished with black and gold threads, while his surcoat hung loosely over his shoulders. I rolled my eyes at his sharp remark.

I swore he only wanted me to attend things like this to humiliate me further. He must have seen me because he leaned forward in his chair, clasping his ringed fingers together on the table while rubbing his thumbs together, which was a motion I recognized when he became angry under the pressure of other royals who may not know about his little secrets.

He looked at me sternly. If looks could catch the world on fire, this castle would have been engulfed. I noticed Gavin take a step forward from the corner of my eye, and my father looked at him for a moment, noticing his shift in movement, and then looked back at me, giving me a look that warned me. My misstep didn't go unnoticed. I was sure he would come up with a way to punish me for it later.

"Now, anyway, where were we?" He gave a look of question to all the other royals around the table. Some I recognized, others I didn't. Anytime we had a ball inviting the other royal kingdoms, we had dinner to offer the other kingdoms insight or opinions on what they wanted for the ball. Drinks, food, entertainment, and so on.

I knew my father only did it to keep the peace, making people feel like they had a say until he could figure out a way to rule all the lands for himself, but they didn't know that. He put on the front of an honest and just king, so anytime I showed disrespect publicly, he didn't take it lightly. He couldn't keep me locked away for his benefit because the kingdoms knew about my mother and me. It would raise too many questions for him he didn't care to deal with, so he let me out of my room for daily walks, mealtimes, and the occasional royal dinner. And of course, the ball we had annually because that was one of the most public events of the year.

Time went by, but eating trenchers before a boring royal dinner filled with monotonous chatter was definitely a bad idea. My eyes felt heavy as I tried to keep my head from nodding off. Pain shot up my leg as Harper stomped my foot under the table with her heel, causing me to jolt upright, making my silverware clink. Nobody seemed to notice. They were all too distracted by a heated conversation about food and table placements. I glanced over to find Gavin looking at his feet, holding back his laugh at catching me dozing off at a royal dinner.

I waited until he had composed himself before I looked back over at him, making a funny face, and we shared a quiet giggle together and then another when I looked back again. Looking at Harper, she shook her head at me as if she already knew what I was planning and was telling me not to do it with the shake of her head.

This time when I looked at Gavin, my eyes were crossed and I stuck my tongue out at him before composing myself again, looking completely unimpressed about anything. He hid his laugh in his arm as he acted like he was coughing, but this time, everyone was looking at me. I heard Harper sigh next to me, and it almost made me lose it, but I held myself together as my father spoke.

"Is there something any of you would like to add?" A flush of heat covered my face and neck, but I kept my voice calm.

"No, I was just telling my knight that I would like to be escorted back to my rooms if that's okay with you, Your Majesty?" I straightened my posture, feeling the tension in my muscles, waiting for his response. He glanced out of the window and noticed that it had already gone dark and was well into the night before waving his hand in dismissal. Harper and I stood as she pushed in our chairs and walked next to me toward the door as Gavin stayed behind us. Harper shut the door behind us and walked forward to let Gavin walk next to me, and I bumped into him with my shoulder and let out a laugh.

"What on earth were you thinking? Are you trying to get yourself hurt?" He looked at me with an emotion in his eyes I had never seen there before. Fear, maybe?

"Gavin, I'm fine. A little defiance hurts nothing other than his ego."

"I've always admired your bravery, Myla, but you're lucky he didn't catch you nodding off! He would've dismissed the table and taken you to the office right then." Harper cut in.

"I guess I'm lucky to have a friend like you who actually pays attention to me, Harp." She rolled her eyes at me and walked ahead.

"And you." I turned my head toward Gavin who was already looking in my direction. "You were looking at me too." He looked away at that, but when he glanced back down at me with those piercing blue eyes and side smile, I felt my legs go weak at the thought of those lips on mine again. His eyes drew me to him. I felt myself leaning toward him without even thinking about it, but the bells pulled me out of my trance as Harper's hand on my arm pulled me away from Gavin. I realized it was the warning bells. The castle was being attacked.

Gavin grabbed my arm and practically pulled me along down the hallways with Harper on our heels, trying to get back to my room. He took the winding stairs two at a time, and I was glad I hadn't worn heels or I would have died as I tried to match his speed. We found the door to my room quickly, and he yanked open the door while Harper and I pooled inside. He came in after us, shutting the door behind him. The sounds of yells of commands came through the balcony door below, along with the sound of armored knights running toward the gates. Gavin pulled me into his chest before leaning down and snatching a dagger from his boot, handing it to me. His hand was laced around the hilt with mine.

"Do you know how to use this?"

"Uh—no, but I think I can figure it out," I said with a heaving breath, my lungs still burning from the run here.

"Take it, stay here, and let nobody in. I'll be back as soon as I can." He urged me towards Harper, but I grabbed his hand, pulling him back to me

"Gavin, wait!" I brought my hand up to cup his cheek. Not caring Harper was standing by, I brought my lips back to his, finishing what almost happened in the hall. He dragged his hand up from the small of my back and rested his hand on the nape of my neck, pulling me in to deepen our kiss for a brief moment before he backed away.

"Aim for the neck or heart." He took off down the hall before turning and yelling back. "Do nothing stupid until I get back," he said with a wink, and I didn't have the chance to tell him anything else. I ran to the balcony to see what was going on. After a moment, I saw Gavin running through the garden to get to the gate. The swords glinted off of the moonlight in the distance as the battle broke out.

I looked back at Gavin, and his eyes met mine. He must have seen my worry as I wrapped my arms around myself, trying to keep calm. I gripped the hilt of the dagger in my hand to keep myself grounded. He gave me a smile that reached his eyes with a slight nod of his head before turning away and storming off into battle with his sword drawn.

I watched from the distance, trying to calm my breathing as my heart raced in my chest until I could no longer see him. I had a bad feeling about this. The kingdom castle had never had an attack against its royal gates. What the hell was happening? I couldn't do this. My chest tightened as I ran to my closet to find my old guard leathers. Harper grabbed my arm.

"What the hell do you think you're doing!?"

"I will not sit here and do nothing," I spat at her

"You do not know what you're doing! You don't know how to fight!"

"I will not let the only man I've ever cared for die out there."

"Gavin can handle himself, Myla. He's a knight, made for war. You're—"

"What, Harp? What—I'm some frail princess who can't handle herself?"

"Myla."

"I might not be rehearsed in battle but I'm not afraid to help someone I care for."

"Myla, please!"

I put on the rest of the leathers, tucked the dagger into my belt, and darted toward the door before she could say another word. I slammed it shut behind me, running to get out of these castle walls and out toward the battle at the gates. Nobody would notice the Princess missing in the midst of all of this chaos.

The warning bells continued, the noise bouncing off the castle walls, ringing in my ears as servants from every direction ran to find safety. The sounds of distant screams and the smell of iron swirled in the air around me as I ran down the spiral stairwell into the vast foyer. I could see the battle in the distance from the French doors. I pushed my strength into my aching legs, preparing to run through the gardens, but I tripped. Not over a rock or fallen branch, but a dead knight, covered in blood, and I froze in place for a moment, feeling rooted to the ground.

This knight was guarding the castle. The battle didn't make it this close inward. How had he ended up dead in cold blood in the gardens? My thought didn't get the chance to finish as a brawny arm wrapped around my neck from behind. Panic thrummed through me as the man spoke.

"You're hard to get a hold of, Princess." He kicked the dead knight on the ground. "He put up quite the fight." He barked a laugh while trying to haul me up off my feet. I pushed against him.

"What do you want with me!?" I screamed, and he squeezed me against him tighter, stilling me while placing his other hand over my mouth. He hissed in my ear.

"Shh, Ferand paid us a pretty coin to come for you." I bit down on his fingers so hard I tasted blood. He yelled, yanking back from me, and then barreled his fist into my face. I saw stars and my head went heavy as I fell to the ground. His enormous hands gripped the collar of my leathers, hauling me up to face him as my hand found the dagger at my waist. I unsheathed it and rammed it into the side of his neck. Blood spurted as the man gargled on a breath before he fell over next to the knight.

The image of his death, I knew, would stay with me forever, but the thought of death finding Gavin made me move, pushing what happened to the back of my mind. I grabbed the sword from the knight's already cold hands. Grasping it with both of my hands, I was surprised by the sheer weight of the thing. How did Gavin swing these around all day when he was training? I used both hands to hold it steady in front of myself, preparing to run head on into the battlefield.

Chapter Seven

GAVIN

The blood of my enemy seeped down my sword, making the hilt harder to grip. He was the third man I had killed at the royal gates tonight, adding his death to the growing number of people I had killed during my lifetime. Another knight brought his sword above his head, swinging his weight down on me. I blocked as he knocked me off balance.

This man was immense, nearly twice my size, but I could use that to my advantage. The bigger they were, the slower they moved. He swung left, right, then jabbed forward with a grunt. I lunged to my left, slashing his side clean open with my blade.

Blood flowed from his wound like a coursing river before I heard the thud of his heavy body landing on the ground.

I saw Roland out of the corner of my eye, taking on two guys on his own. I rushed to his aid, slaying one man straight through the opening between his rear cuirass plate and pauldron, sending my blade straight through his heart and out through his other side. Bringing my foot to the center of his back, I unsheathed his body from my blade before moving to the next one.

"Nice of you to finally show up, brother." Roland tilted his head down to me while throwing his arms out, looking at me through narrowed eyes before bringing his sword down against another man swinging toward him. This guy was smaller and more scrawny than the others I had seen. He seemed young, but I couldn't see his face through his helmet. Roland kicked his foot into his chest, knocking him to the ground.

"Let me take a guess." He turned to me now as if he weren't worried about the battle happening around us. "You were with the Princess?" He grabbed a small blade from his side, throwing it right past me, sticking it directly into the eye of the man behind me that was holding a sword over my head, readying to strike.

"The same Princess that you were supposed to extinguish those feelings for." The man from behind me fell over and reminded me why I had never liked to be on Roland's bad side. He rushed to me as we walked forward past the gates, pushing the enemies back beyond the crown's land. The action made my chest loosen from knowing the enemy was being pushed further away from

Myla. There had never been a direct attack on the castle gates until tonight.

"Her name is Myla, and I think the flame is turning into a wildfire". He rolled his eyes at the metaphorical terms of our conversation before turning away, dodging a man's strike. He cleaved his sword down, severing his arm. The man cried out before falling to the ground in pain. The thought of Myla made me look back toward the castle where I left her. I wondered why these men would attack the castle gates head on. It was a suicide mission. Looking back, my heart dropped to the pits of my stomach as I realized what this battle was. A distraction.

No leader would send men to the front lines of kingdom walls for anything else. I felt the blood drain from my face. I knew I must have been completely pallid by the time Roland turned toward me again because he looked at me with wild eyes before rushing forward.

"Gavin!" he roared from across the way, but it was too late. The searing pain of a dagger's blade pierced my side through my leathers. Slamming my elbow into the enemy's nose behind me, I knocked him away while Roland landed the finishing blow.

I ran forward, glaring at the castle garden in the distance, my eyes unable to believe what they were seeing. Too focused on her to feel the pain throbbing through my side, I thought I was picturing Myla in my mind's eye. But I wasn't picturing her. She was here. In the middle of a battlefield. Her eyes finally caught sight of mine through the scarce trees. My run turned into a sprint toward her. What the hell was she doing out here?! What was she thinking? How did she get a sword?

I reached her quickly, pushing her behind one of the larger trees, shielding us from view. She threw her arms around me, dropping her weapon. She had caught me by surprise. Her eyes brimmed with tears, but she held them back as she rambled.

"I'm sorry. I couldn't just stay. I—I was so worried. I thought—" She placed my face in between the palms of her hands. Bringing my forehead down to hers, I savored the warmth of her touch against me. She thought the worst and came out here. A royal. A princess who shouldn't care about my very existence ran into a battlefield, blade drawn, to be sure I was okay. My heart melted into the pits of my chest at the thought.

The desire to erase all distance between us took over. I pulled my lips to hers and I wrapped my arms around her in an unbreakable hold, never wanting her to leave the safety of them again. Bringing my hands up to her face, I pulled her deeper into our kiss. She opened her mouth further for me as our tongues glided gracefully over one another's.

I pushed her back against the tree; her soft lips moved in rhythm with my own. A pleasing little hum of pleasure escaped her. The sound drove me absolutely mad. My hand fisted into her long black curls at her nape. She ran her hands down my sides and then up my back, drawing me closer to her. The pulsating pain in my side returned, and I winced in between our passionate kisses.

She drew back with her eyes still hooded from pleasure, but they soon filled with concern at seeing the blood on her hands.

"Oh my god, Gavin, you're bleeding." Her eyes went frantic, searching for the wound leaking at my side. I grabbed her hands. She was trembling either at the sight of my blood on her hands or from the pleasure of our encounter.

"Uh, hello, Gavin! We're still, oh I don't know, in the middle of a battle!" Roland shouted from a few yards away, fighting off the last of the invaders with other knights of Baela backing him. I unsheathed my sword, wrapping my arm around Myla, tugging her behind me.

"Stay behind me." Myla picked up her sword off the ground on shaky legs. She followed my steps forward. Two invaders raced toward us. I thrust my sword, grounding my stance, and started the dance of blades with them. We dodged and struck, dodged and struck, dodged and struck until one tired out enough that he missed his mark and I took him down first. The second tried rushing me, but before I got the chance to swing, he already had a sword through his chest.

He fell to his knees, eyes wide with shock, before gargling on his last breath. Myla was standing behind him as she let go of the sword, letting the lifeless man fall to the ground. She had speared him, had killed him. Her eyes were blazing with astonishment. I knew mine mirrored the same because the Princess of Baela killed a man to protect me. Roland walked over, bent at the waist, trying to catch his breath. He put his hands on his knees.

"Well, I've never seen a princess kill a man in guard leathers and a tiara." He huffed out a laugh. "She seems fun, Gavin. You could use more of that in your life; maybe you should keep her around." He smacked my back hard, making me lose my footing.

"Well, I have never been aroused on a battlefield before, so today was a first for many things, I suppose." I spoke, smirking at Myla. Her cheeks flushed red and I didn't hide the smile tugging at my lips. Roland put his hands up in the air like I had caught him.

"I can't concur with that one." He looked at both of us with a shrug as his smile slowly stretched over his features, and Myla and I didn't hold back our laugh at his admission. "What? We were at war for a long time, mate. A man's gotta do what a man's gotta do." I shook my head at him, grinning while turning back to Myla.

This woman ran out into battle with no regard for her own safety, again, to make sure I was alright, and I had never been so pissed and in awe of something in my entire life. I placed my hand on her lower back, guiding her back to the castle, walking past Roland as he helped our men gather the bodies of the fallen and wounded. "I'll see you at the mess hall in the morning," I said.

"Oh, I'm sure you will.'' He glanced at Myla and then back at me, and I kept walking with Myla by my side. I accompanied her back through the gate, making our way through the paths of the garden in silence. A part of me wanted to yell at her for putting herself in such danger, but the other part of me wanted to hold her and be thankful that she was okay. As I ushered her on, my adrenaline wound down and my heartbeat slowed.

The pain stretched through my side with every stride. My muscles ached and slowed me down. Myla noticed my sluggish pace as we approached the stairs leading up to her tower, and she wrapped her arm around me to help me along.

"Gavin, are you going to be alright?" She placed her hand over my injury, squeezing to apply pressure while we walked up the stairs. I nodded my head toward her. Each step was grueling; the spiraling staircase made me feel uneasy as we climbed them one step at a time. The muscles in my legs were gnawing at me to stop by the time we finally made it up the steps. I could see the shadowed spots caving in around my line of sight as we approached Mylas door. It swung open and Harper was there, but she didn't have time to say anything before Myla gave her orders.

"He's lost some blood. He's weak. Get more bandages and alcohol—help me get him to the bed." Her voice sounded muffled and far away as I tried to focus on my surroundings. The clanking of the metal and flashes of war fluttered through my mind. My heart raced, my palms grew sweaty, and I squeezed my eyes shut. Harper handed me a skin of water when I opened them again. The sight of her familiar face pulled me back to now while Myla tended to my side. She poured some pungent liquid over it, and it instantly jolted me back to my senses.

"Gavin, lift your arm so I can help you." I winced but held my composure as the burning sensation lingered from the alcohol she dumped on it. She pulled off my leather pads and tunic before examining my side.

"You're going to need some stitches," she said while pulling out a needle and thread.

"Do it." I lifted my arm above my head and gripped the headboard, watching her as she took her thread, tying it into a tight knot around the needle with her teeth before dousing it with alcohol. She sent the small needle weaving in and out of my skin until the gash was nothing but a thin line.

"How did you learn how to do this?" She didn't meet my eyes with her response, and I immediately regretted asking the question.

"Let's just say I've had wounds of my own." She grabbed a small glass jar with some type of salve inside it, rubbing it along the closed wound

"This will help with the pain while it heals."

"It's fine, really. I've had pain worse than this." Grimacing, I tried to ease my tensed muscles. She just rolled her eyes at my stubborn show of masculine strength before setting it on the small table next to the bed.

"I'm going to give you guys some time. I'll be back tomorrow, Myla," Harper spoke and quickly made her way to the door before Myla could say anything to her. Furrowing my brow, I asked,

"Are you two all right?"

"Yeah, I think she's just upset at me for running off like I did."

"I can't blame her. You scared the shit out of me out there, Myla." She looked up to me at that.

"Yeah, well, I don't want you running off fighting your battles alone, so teach me."

"What?"

"Teach me how to fight. I don't want to be some defenseless damsel anymore. I want to learn." She looked at me with eyes of anticipation, almost as if she expected me to tell her no.

Thinking about it, it would benefit not only me being the one protecting her, but it could give her the confidence to stand up against her father's grueling punishments if she knew how to fight back. She let out a sigh while looking down. Rising to her feet, she started walking toward the bathing chamber.

"I'll run you some water so you can get cleaned up," she said, sounding defeated.

"Wait... Okay."

"Okay... what?"

"I'll teach you."

Her eyes brightened at that, and it brought a side smile to my face. She bounced on her toes before rushing off to the bathing chamber to run some water. I got up to follow her in there, the cream already numbing the pain in my side. I walked up behind her, my hand slid around her waist, and she flinched at the surprising touch.

"Sorry," I whispered. "I didn't mean to scare you." It broke my heart that even a touch made her flinch in fear. How many times had the touch from another person caused her pain rather than give tender affection or pleasure?

"No, no, it's fine. Here." She handed me a towel and a change of clothes. Harper must have grabbed them from somewhere before she left. "I'll let you clean up this time." She walked out of the room and shut the door behind her, but it took everything in me not to go out there and drag her back in here with me.

Chapter Eight

Myla

It was my turn to take a bath after Gavin got out, but seeing him walk out of my bathing chamber in nothing but a towel, still dripping from the tub, tied my stomach into knots, making a fire ignite within me. He grabbed the pants Harper had found for him that were folded at the end of the bed, but we couldn't take our eyes off of each other from the moment he stepped out of that room. I wondered what he was thinking when he looked at me like that. With his stare filled with eager intention, I forced myself to look away and walk out onto the balcony to get some air.

I needed some air. Air that neither of us were sharing because I felt like I couldn't breathe. This man made me breathless in the best of ways that I'd never felt before. The light of the morning was already shining over the horizon, filling the sky with bright pinks and orange hues of light. It was beautiful, really. I had always loved the beauty of the world I lived in, but sometimes it was hard to acknowledge it when my life had always been filled with the darkness of my punishments hovering above me like a storm cloud.

A few moments passed before I heard the balcony door open behind me. Gavin's warm, crisp scent hit me with the next passing breeze, and my breath hitched in my throat. His hand touched my lower back before he spoke.

"I ran a fresh bath for you, Your Highness." There it was, back to the honorable knight with the formal titles. I turned around in his light hold and ran into his bare, muscled chest. He cleaned up his side and wrapped a bandage around his abdomen, but I could still see all of his defined muscles built from war. His hair was still damp, making it fall over his brow instead of it being swept out of his face like it normally was. His eyes were piercing into my very soul.

I cleared my throat, trying to control the growing desire rooting deep in my gut for this man. I swore that if I stayed out here any longer, I'd give him all of me right here, but I knew deep down I could never be with him, no matter how much I wanted to be. A royal princess being with a lowly knight was forbidden. My father would never allow it. He'd probably kill me for not wanting to be with a man of royalty and high status in our society. Gavin pulled me back to reality when his warm hand that was placed on my back fell away, back down to his side. It was almost like he knew where my thoughts had gone.

I couldn't bear looking into those beautiful eyes of his a moment longer. I pushed myself off the cool stone of the balcony wall he had me pinned against. Moving past him, I marched straight to the bathing chamber, shutting the door behind me. Not daring to look behind me, I could feel Gavin's eyes burning into my back the whole time.

I tried to be quick, taking off the leathers and dipping myself down into the tub. I tried to scrub the blood and dirt of the battlefield off of me to prepare myself for tomorrow, well, today now. But the thought of the men I killed would haunt me for the rest of my life. I killed people tonight. I slipped down further into the tub, resting my head against the edge.

Gavin had run the bath for me. His kind gesture made me smile to myself. I lathered the soap in my hair and rinsed it before doing the same with my body. I scrubbed until it ached, making sure I had gotten everything off. Relaxing against the warmth of the water, I could feel myself nodding off from the stress subsiding within me.

The darkness consumed me; the walls fell in around me as I saw one of the men I had killed covered in blood and lying lifeless at my feet. Glimpses of Harper looking at me with the same disdain all the other royals had shown me my whole life circled around me. Everyone's judgmental stares followed me as I fell to my knees. Upon closer inspection, it wasn't the man I had killed that was dead at my feet, and I turned him over to see his face. It was the only man I cared about. A scream worked through my throat as warm hands pulled me from the now cold, murky water I was submerged in.

"Myla." His soothing voice pulled me back to reality, and when I opened my eyes, his face was inches from mine. His arms were holding me up out of the water I was sitting in. Chills prickled over the skin above the water. My breathing was heavy.

"Are you alright? I heard you scream." My senses slowly came back to me, and I realized Gavin was shirtless, holding my naked body in my bathtub, and I quickly grabbed a towel. Standing, I wrapped it around myself. Shame rose within me. Gavin was once again a witness to my nakedness. Not just physically, but emotionally as he pulled me from the depths of it.

Guilt rose next for the men I had killed and for Harper being frustrated with me. But also because the moment Gavin got hurt was when his eyes found mine on the battlefield. I didn't know the extension of the damage until his blood coated my hands. My racing thoughts made my chest heavy as I stepped out of the tub. My eyes burned from the emotions bubbling behind them. I was unable to fight the tears that slowly slipped down my face. For a moment, Gavin stood there like a silent anchor before he stepped forward and wrapped his powerful arms around me. I wanted to form words, but the only thing I could manage was an apology.

"I'm sorry." I sobbed into his chest as he clasped one hand tightly around me while running the other through my damp hair.

"I'm so sorry," I rasped between shaky breaths. "I killed them."

"Shhh" was the only sound that came from his lips as he consoled me. He held me until my sobs turned into shallow breaths.

"Let's get you to bed." He took a step back, grabbing my nightgown that was set to the side for me. He grabbed my hands, lifting my arms above my head so he could slide the nightgown over my body. His eyes never left mine. Liquid heat pooled in my center; desire replaced the dull ache left in my chest.

I let the towel fall to the floor as the nightgown flowed just over my thighs. His eyes roamed over like he was imagining what was under my gown, even though he already knew. He picked me up, carried me to the bed, cradled against his warm chest, and it brought me back to the memory of our first kiss. I glanced at his lips before looking to the bed where a tray lay, the smell reminding me of some type of sweet bread.

I didn't know if Gavin had learned from Harper that one of my weaknesses was bread, but if he was trying to lure me further, it was working. He sat me on the bed next to the small tray of food, and it looked like a bowl of heady stew and bread, before he moved to the end of the bed, where a fresh tunic was laid out for him.

"Harper stopped by with food, and I asked her for some clean clothes, but I think she was really just wanting to check in on you," he said to me while I sat up on the bed. He pulled on the clean tunic and his leathers. A small frown pulled on my face from his muscled frame being hidden from me by clothes.

Within minutes, he was back in his light leathers, sitting on the chair in the corner and putting his boots back on. He leaned back, grabbing the trinket that was sitting on my nightstand next to him. He inspected the opened locket closely. I recognized it the moment he picked it up. It was sentimental to me. Gavin was running his fingers over the etched carving of vines and flowers circling around the locket in a whimsical design.

"It was my mother's" was the first thing I mustered up the strength to say, and he looked up to me and then back to the locket before running one of his hands through his hair and setting it back down.

"Were you close to her?" he asked.

"Yes, I remember when she gave me that locket. It was one of the last memories I had with her." I clasped my hands together in front of me to keep myself from fidgeting. "Every morning when we would go on our morning walk after breakfast, we would walk through the gardens together."

"I'm sorry, Myla."

"It's alright; it was a long time ago. Now it's my turn."

"What do you mean?"

"A question for a question." I looked at him, smiling at his furrowed brow. "You asked me a question. Now it's my turn to ask you one."

"You can ask whatever you like while we're training."

"Training? Here? Now? Aren't you tired?" I asked.

"Yes, but it's daybreak which means I'm off duty, so if you want to learn, this would be the only time to do it. We can do a lesson every morning." My smile beamed across my face at his words.

"Unless you're not up for it today after everything that happened."

"No I am, but what about your side?" I asked him.

"I'll live, and that's five questions now, so I believe it's my turn."

"That's not fair." He released a warm laugh that made my heart melt into a puddle before continuing.

"Okay, fine, stand here." He pulled me to the center of the room before going into the bathing chamber, and he came out holding the dagger that was still strapped to my leathers. "Take this." I grabbed the hilt of the dagger to hold it.

"I don't get to learn with a sword?"

"A sword is too heavy for you right now. We'll start with the dagger. Legs shoulder width apart, arms up, ground yourself." He took his stance, giving me a visual to go off of.

"Like this?" I asked.

"Straighten your posture." I straightened and stood there, already feeling the minor aches in my muscles that I had never used from correcting my stance alone. "Now, breathe in then exhale and thrust it forward like you're going to attack. Like this." He moved next to me, unsheathed his sword, and moved so quickly I barely registered the steps he took.

My pulse fluttered as my imagination got the best of me—I imagined Gavin in nothing but the towel he was in earlier teaching me swordplay fresh out of the bath. My eyes roamed over his body, admiring his rippling muscles against his snug leathers. I shook away the thought and cleared my throat. His eyes were on me now. I did as he said, taking in a breath, then out. I moved the blade forward, but my dagger's motion was weak compared to his example.

"That was good for a first try. Now try this." He got back into his fighting stance, did a squat, came up, and thrust forward. "This will strengthen your muscles and help you better control your movements. Switch the blade to the other hand after every strike."

"How long am I supposed to do this?"

"Let's do a set of ten, for now. Wouldn't want you to overdo it."

"Oh, come on, it can't be that bad. I want to do more. Learn more."

"Okay, then do as many as you want and I'll teach you a new stance in a few days." He walked toward the door. The thought of him leaving made me panic, so I didn't stop myself from trying to get him to stay.

"Wait, you don't have to go yet—maybe you could escort me down to breakfast or we could go for a walk in the gardens. I'm allowed a morning walk in the gardens..." As my voice broke over my words, I felt the heat rise within me. I had no right to ask him to stay, but I didn't want him to leave. I looked down at my feet, feeling embarrassed at what I must have looked like begging my knight not to leave me alone. The warmth of his palm on my cheek brought my eyes back to his. He was cautious of my bruised face.

"Do you want me to stay?" he asked softly.

"Yes," I whispered.

"Okay, one condition."

"Anything,"

"Do another set." He smiled And I laughed at his request as he brought his hand back down to his side. He moved over to my bed and got comfortable, taking off his tunic and lying on the bed wearing nothing but his trousers. I walked over to my closet and pulled out a silky pair of pants for bed to wear under my nightgown while I did the last set he asked for. I looked over at him lying down with his eyes on me.

"You're going to watch me?" I asked with a tilt of my head.

"I'm the judge who will give you constructive criticism." The last of his words came out sensual as he sat back on the bed, lifting a brow. I rolled my eyes at him but got into position.

"Where are you from?" I asked, trying to get back to our question for a question game.

"A small farm town on the outskirts of Baela." I counted the movements in my head.

One, down two, up, three thrust, switch.

"What about you? Have you ever been anywhere outside of the royal grounds?" he asked.

"No, never." He shook his head at my response as if it were sad, but I wouldn't know what life was like beyond these walls, so I had never thought of it as a somber situation, but I had always been curious about what lied beyond these walls.

"Do you have any siblings?"

"Yes, two younger brothers and a baby sister, or at least she was a baby to me. She was just a child when I left for the war almost seven years ago. I haven't been home since."

"Oh gosh, Gavin, I'm sorry. Have you talked to your family through the mail at least?"

"My question, my turn."

"Fine," I rolled my eyes again with a half smile. He took a sweet roll from the tray next to him as if he were trying to tease me with the food, taking a bite out of the buttery bread before continuing,

"If you could go anywhere, where would you want to go?"

"The ocean. I've always wanted to see it for myself. I've heard it's beautiful."

One, down two, up, three thrust, switch. I kept counting my movements in my head. I was almost done.

"You wouldn't be wrong."

"You've seen it?"

"Yes, the town I'm from is close to the ocean."

"I bet it's lovely there." I looked out toward my balcony window, and the sun began peeking, and I imagined I could see the waves crashing along the beach. I paused my exercise.

"Gavin." I looked at him. "Why haven't you been home? The war has been over for a while now." Gavin's jaw pulsed and he looked away from me. He shook his head softly, like he was struggling to find the right words, trying to decide if he wanted to answer or not, and I wished I could take back the question.

"My father and I both went to war, only I made it. I haven't been home because I don't know if I can face my mother after what happened."

Before he finished his answer, I was next to him on the bed.

"You cannot blame yourself for that, Gavin." I placed my hand on his cheek, pulling his gaze to mine. "You will go home one day, you will see your mother, and I promise you she will welcome you home with open arms."

"And how could you possibly know that?"

"Because she's your mother."

He cleared his throat and pulled away from me.

"My turn," he said while moving the food to the side table and lying down on the bed, making himself more comfortable.

"What were you truly doing the night we met outside the gates?" I hesitated a moment but told him anyway.

"I take leftover food and medicine to the townspeople in need. They get word to Harper and then I sneak out to deliver it to them." He laughed.

"So that's where the apple came from." He smiled warmly at me and flutters floated to my chest. "No rodents I take it then?" he asked with a tone filled with amusement, and I couldn't stop my laugh. His features grew more serious. His jaw ticked as he looked at me. Arctic eyes filled with something I'd never seen before met mine. "You never cease to amaze me, Princess" His words caused my cheeks to burn from the intensity of his stare. I averted his gaze, glancing out the balcony doors again.

"My turn." I tried not to stumble over my words. "What's your favorite color?" I continued nervously, answering my question. "I love the sky at sunrise and sunset, if those count as favorite colors..." I trailed off, and he gave me a half smile with a loud, tired sigh as he sunk further into my bed.

"Hmmm, mine's blue," he answered, closing his eyes. "Are the royal beds always this comfortable?" he asked.

"I've never slept in another bed, so I wouldn't know any different."

"Maybe I should stay in your bed more often." He glanced at me with a sleepy smile, giving me a wink, and I felt the blood rush to my cheeks again at the way he looked at me. He was sleepy-eyed with his tousled hair, and I smiled back, forcing myself to get up to go to the bathing chamber to splash some water on my face to clean up.

I tried to get the burning desire to subside before going back into the bedroom. The cool water awakened my senses; my skin pebbled. Once I regained my composure and walked back out, Gavin was already peacefully asleep on my bed. Sir Gavin was asleep. In my bed. Shirtless. I crawled into bed beside him and watched the rise and fall of his chest as he slept soundlessly.

Why I was so drawn to this man, I did not know, but we had shared two heated encounters now and I wasn't sure how to handle the desires I had for him. I looked him over, seeing his scars from the war. Some were more faded than others, but the man had been through more than one battle in his lifetime.

The one I noticed the most was the one over his chest. It was bigger and more jagged than the others. I could tell it was a severe wound based on how it looked. I rolled over closer to him, even though I knew I shouldn't.

I knew little about Gavin, but the thought of never meeting him saddened me. Before I met him in the garden that night, all I was, was a prisoner with a crown, a nobody, a pawn in my father's rule of the kingdoms. Nobody noticed me or paid me any attention, but every time Gavin and I were in the same room, it was as if we were the only ones there. He saw me for all that I was and still wanted to be around me. Still wanted me. He rolled in my direction, wrapping me in his arms, and I closed my eyes while taking in a heady breath of his scent. He smelled like spring after heavy rain and something else that was smooth and woodsy. I couldn't place it.

I didn't want to wake him as I tried to pull myself back, but he pulled me in, and I felt myself relax in his embrace, fitting in the nook of his arms perfectly. I knew that whatever this was between us needed to stop before anyone found out about it, but I couldn't help the want I had to be with him—around him.

"Goodnight, Myla." His warm breath brushed my neck with his soft words, making me relax further into him.

"Goodnight, Gavin." He held me a little tighter before his breathing became deep and even with sleep. The comfort of his arms was something I had never experienced before, and I never wanted this feeling to end. Soon I felt my eyelids grow heavy, and I reveled in the warmth of his embrace as I drifted to sleep.

I jolted awake at the bedroom door swinging open, and so did Gavin. Harper was standing in the doorway with her mouth agape, staring at us with disbelief in her eyes, and I quickly noticed why. Gavin was shirtless next to me, and we were intertwined in each other's arms in the middle of the day.

"Oh, my gods! Myla!" Harper squealed while Gavin leaped out of the bed quickly, trying to throw on his tunic and leathers as Harper narrowed in on him.

"Did you—"

"Harp," I yelled at her while shaking my head. "It's not what you think," I said hastily. "We fell asleep, nothing more." Harper darted her gaze to me, crossing her arms over her chest. She looked down a moment, muttering under her breath, thanking the gods for something before bringing her eyes back to Gavin and me.

"Look, I'm all for you two being—" She looked between the two of us. "—whatever this is that is happening between you here, but you need to be careful." She looked to Gavin. "The King is not a good man; he has taken heads for far less." Gavin looked down as Harper looked to me now. "And not to mention the punishment—" Harper shook her head, not letting her mind go there as Gavin looked at me with a furrowed brow, sorrow filled his eyes as if he felt ashamed at the thought of what my father would do to me if he found out about this connection between us. It balled a knot of emotion in my throat.

Not being able to spend time with Gavin would be devastating. When I was around him, I felt like I wasn't so lost in the shadows of my so-called royal life. Like the King didn't keep me trapped within the walls of my tower. I knew Harper was trying to be a good friend, and I knew she was worried for my well-being, but I was beginning to wonder if these feelings I had for Gavin could be stopped. Even by my father.

Gavin sat on the bench at the end of the bed and laced up his brown leather boots while Harper changed the subject, rambling about the ball again.

"I can't wait to see you in your dress, Myla! You're going to look stunning. I picked the perfect dress today." She squealed happily this time while sitting next to me on the bed. Gavin stood and started heading towards the door, almost like he thought he could slip out unnoticed by Harper.

"Gavin," Harper called to him, "don't keep a lady waiting for the ball." He looked to me at her comment with his soul-piercing gaze.

"I'd never keep her waiting." He gave me that side smile of his that made finches fly in my stomach, not butterflies; the light flutter of their wings did not compare to the way Gavin made me feel. "Princess," he said with a nod of his head to me before turning and walking out of the room.

When the door shut behind him, it was as if my surroundings came back into focus. I wrapped my arms around my knees and sat there in silence for a moment, not wanting to interrupt the memory playing back of being in Gavin's arms. Harper cleared her throat, and when I looked over at her, she was giving me a look that was telling me to spill all the tea, and I couldn't help but laugh at her.

"All we did was sleep, Harp."

"Mhm, keep telling yourself you're not falling in love with that man and it might come true." I looked away from her at that, knowing that deep down, it was true. No matter how hard I tried to deny it, I was falling in love with Sir Gavin Dawson.

The thoughts of my admiration for Gavin got interrupted when the door busted open as the man on my mind hurried himself back into my room with fear-filled eyes.

Chapter Nine

Gavin

"It's Frederick. He's coming up the stairwell." Myla's scared eyes darted to Harper, who placed her hand over her chest as if trying to catch her breath from what I'd said.

"Hide!" Myla leaped from the bed to grab my arm and pulled me over to Harper, who already held the closet door open for me before she pushed me inside, slamming it in my face. The bedroom door creaked as it swung open, and I listened against the closet door as Frederick's heavy boots walked into the room.

"Princess," he crooned. I could hear the smile in his tone.

"What do you want?" Myla questioned, but I had a good idea of what he was doing here. Myla left the castle, rushed into battle, and she had the bruise on her cheek which didn't help her case if she tried to deny it.

"I think you already know." His voice sounded doubtless, unwavering even though the door muffled the conversation. Silence hung between them a moment. Myla didn't speak, didn't deny, and I imagined she hung her head, knowing there was no fighting the punishment that was certain to be coming. I heard the boots against the hard floors and the creak of the door again before Harper started pleading for her friend.

"Fredrick, please... Don't—" The sound of a hand smacking flesh and Harper's cry echoed in the room. I had to fight the urge to burst through the closed door.

"Harper, it's okay. I'll be fine." Her voice was stern, strong, but I could hear the uncertainty behind it. I huffed out a breath of frustration, trying to restrain myself. She was so brave. How long had this been going on? The respect I had for Myla grew daily, along with the wildfire of emotions for her in my chest.

Our places in court would never permit us to be together, but that had never stopped my endless thoughts of her throughout the days since she stumbled into my life. She had even haunted my dreams. Everything about her, her warmth, her scent, engulfed me daily, and I didn't think anyone could put out the fire.

I didn't want her to endure this pain anymore. The door to her room slammed and the eerie quiet soaked into me through the walls. I waited a beat of my heart before I opened the door and found Harper in the large chair in the corner. A single tear lingered on her cheek.

"Hey," I murmured, but she still jumped and turned to me.

"Oh, sorry!" She quickly wiped the tear from her reddened face from where Frederick had hit her before standing. She then returned to her normal self. "You better go. I'll come get you when he brings her back. I'm assuming he won't call you for her escort since you're off duty until tonight." She sniffled, and my previous thought came back to me.

I did not want Myla to endure this pain, and I'd rather take it for myself than see her hurt again, lying in a cold tub of murky water, screaming from the nightmares. My jaw ticked, and my fists clenched. I refused to let her endure that again. Harper took notice of my stillness.

"What is it?" she questioned. "What's wrong?"

"I'm going to volunteer myself in Myla's place." It was the first thing I said to her from all my spiraling thoughts. Her eyes filled with panic again, her mouth agape.

"Gavin, you can't! They'll kill you! Myla will live. He wouldn't kill her. She's too valuable to him. He can use her as his political pawn any way he pleases, and he knows that. But you're just a knight. He wouldn't think twice about killing you. If anything, them knowing you and Myla know each other would make him inflict more damage to hurt her further."

"I don't care!" My voice raised. Harper took a step back from me as I lost my temper. "I will not stand by and watch the pain she went through again." Harper shook her head.

"So better it be you than her?" she questioned before continuing, "Either way she gets hurt. She wouldn't want you to do this, Gavin. If anything happened—" I cut off her words.

"I'll take on the pain for her if it keeps her unharmed, and I'll deal with her guilt for it later. The only thing that matters to me is her." Harper huffed out a breath as her lips curled slightly on the sides.

"What?" I asked

"You're falling in love with her...." She said it almost more to herself than to me, but her words made me straighten, and I held my breath. I had never admitted that truth to myself out loud. A moment lingered between us before I darted for the door. I left Harper standing there with the silence of my confession.

I made it to the long corridor that led to the King's office from where Myla stumbled out last time. My breathing was heavy from the sprint here, but I yelled down the hall to where Fredrick and Myla stood in front of the large doors leading to what I presumed was a torture chamber of sorts for the King.

"Wait!" I hastily made my way down the hall just as the door thudded open and the King stepped out. His dark features were even darker from the shadows behind the door. Myla looked at me with weary eyes. The emotion behind them made my heart shatter, and my chest constricted. I didn't know how many more of these punishments her soul could take before she broke. Moving my eyes from hers to the King, I kneeled before him, although I felt like burying him where he stood.

"Your Majesty, I volunteer." I spoke effortlessly; no hesitation rang in my tone. I was sure I would take on anything for the Princess, who had always taken on everything for everyone else. Her heart was for her people, her kingdom, in anything she did, and it made pride swell within me. Myla was a light that glowed brighter than any flame, and I refused to let this king take that from her.

"Excuse me?" His voice sounded surprised. "Volunteer for what, exactly?"

"For Myla's punishment. Whatever it is, I want to take her place."

"No!" Myla cried out, and Frederick held her back from lurching toward me.

"Hmmm." The King contemplated a moment, but I knew he had decided when he saw the panic lingering on Myla's face from my offer. A wicked, crooked smile curved on his lips as he looked back at me.

"Very well," he said with a wave of a hand, and Frederick pushed Myla to the ground and grabbed me by the arms, shoving them behind my back and gripping them there.

"Gavin! No! Please!" Myla cried as her body crashed into mine in a soul-crushing hug. She squeezed me with all her strength, and I buried my head into the crook of her neck, savoring her touch, her scent, if only for a moment—wildflowers and spring. As if she had taken so many walks in the garden, the smell clung to her. The embrace lasted a moment before the King yanked her off of me and pushed her down the hall, dismissing her.

"Father, please..." she begged with tear-smeared eyes.

"Leave us." King Henry spoke with unquestioned authority while turning back to Frederick, leading us into his chambers. I tried to crane my neck over my shoulder to glimpse at Myla, but Frederick pushed me harder, forcing me to look straight ahead. I heard the door close with a thud, and Myla's cries echoed down the hall. I prepared myself for what was to come. I knew that whatever pain was waiting for me, it was worth it, for her. That was the only thing I was sure of as I heard the crack of a whip. The all-consuming pain coursed through me as warm blood trailed down my back.

Chapter Ten

Myla

Twenty-one. I sobbed harder after every crack I heard echoing down the hall. The sound made my whole body shudder. The most I had ever remembered enduring was ten, eleven at the most. But Gavin endured twenty-one lashes for me.

My chest ached to the point of being unable to breathe. The guilt I had weighed me down like lead in my chest, pulling me under the dark waters to drown in my misery. I was sure my father knew I'd heard everything and lapped it up like a starved animal. They drew every lash out. Henry took his time. The King knew I wouldn't leave. I couldn't. My heart would never let me.

After the eleventh crack, Gavin's groans of pain had all but gone quiet.

I called for a servant to send word to Roland. I didn't give any details other than the Princess needed his assistance. He showed up shortly after, and when he saw the condition I was in, sitting up against the wall of the long hall on the ground, he looked at me with knowing eyes and a shake of his head. We waited silently together on the cold, hard floor for three more cracks before Roland wrapped an arm around my shoulder and pulled me into him.

I lost it on that fourteenth lash. I wanted to scream, but no sound escaped me. Just endless tears as I slumped into him, accepting his comfort as my shoulders quaked and my chest caved inward. I tried to swallow down the boulder in my throat to articulate words, but my voice sounded broken.

"He took my place," I whimpered, but Roland just squeezed me tighter, trying to remain strong. But even I could hear the emotion in his voice.

"It'll be okay... He'll be okay," he whispered, his voice dry, but I just shook my head.

"It's too much... They're going to—"

"No." Roland cut off my words before I had the chance to finish them. "Don't say that. Gavin's strong; he'll make it through this." I nodded, doing my best to put faith into his words. Into Gavin. But a man's body could only handle so much. By the last crack of the whip, my eyes stared distantly at my feet, empty, dull. I cradled my legs, pulled them up to my chest. Cold, I was so cold. As if I had cried so hard my limbs lost all feeling in them.

The only thing I felt was the warmth of Roland's body next to mine and the steady, throbbing pain in my chest. When the door thudded open, Frederick tossed Gavin to the ground like he was nothing more than trash. My father stepped forward holding a glass of amber liquor, taking a long sip, standing next to his servant before giving me a wicked, curved smile, not a hair out of place on him. You wouldn't have thought he'd tortured a man moments before.

He tapped his rings against his glass, and Frederick understood the command with no words being spoken between them. They walked past us, stepping over Gavin's limp body like he was nothing more than a stump in their path. As their footsteps receded down the hall, we rushed to Gavin. Roland hauled him up to his feet, placing Gavin's arm over his shoulder, and I mimicked his actions on Gavin's other side.

"Gavin. Gavin, please." I tried to talk to him as we stumbled him down the hall, and I got no response, which only made the panic in me rise further.

"Myla, he's breathing. He'll make it."

"You don't know that!" I raised my voice at him, but it didn't seem to phase him.

"The man's too stubborn to die. Isn't that right, mate?" He gave Gavin a small nudge and he let out a mumble in response. Roland smiled

"Told ya, there he is." I kept up as we almost made it to the end of the hall, and I couldn't help that the small grumble upturned my lips. A small sign he was still somewhat conscious had made me feel better. Rounding the corner, Henry and Frederick stood there, chatting about something before my father turned to me.

"Myla." He smiled. "Remember, don't leave the castle." I looked at Roland

"It's alright. I got him. I'll get him to the knights' quarters," Roland said.

"I'll help you to the garden doors," I said hastily as we passed my father and Frederick, watching us smugly. I gave them a menacing look before we continued on, passing a few servants with curious eyes, but most evaded us as we dragged Gavin along, eventually making it to the garden foyer. The chatter about what happened would spread quickly.

I stood and watched Roland carry the weight Gavin couldn't as they stumbled through the garden. They were completely out of my view before I went back to my room. I knew I wouldn't be able to sneak out tonight. I was sure my father would have extra eyes on me after what had happened. But I was determined to get to Gavin when I had the chance.

A week went by and the only communication I had with Gavin was through Roland and Harper relaying our messages to each

other. Giving me updates on how he was doing. The last message being that Gavin had been moving around better and that he missed my bed. When Harper gave me her flirty side smile with the message, I couldn't help the picture of Gavin giving me his smirk and a playful wink.

That image ran through my mind on repeat. Through the days since the punishment, I had been stealing vials of medicine to help with his pain and his wounds, handing them off to Harper to give to Roland in passing. It wasn't really stealing since the castle nurse knew me well enough at this point. Every time she saw me, I could see the pity in her eyes. She'd give whatever I needed freely as long as she could get away with it without losing her job.

Turning away from her gaze, I shoved some of the medicinal salves and elixirs into the pockets of my dress and left swiftly, giving her a nod of my head, and she left me with a hopeful smile. I made my way back to my room, my hands growing clammy from nerves. Tonight, I planned to sneak to the knights' quarters to see Gavin.

I had waited long enough. I shut my bedroom door behind me, and Harper sat in my large reading chair in the corner. Her eyes shot over to me as she jumped from the sudden sound. She had been on edge all day ever since I told her I would sneak out tonight to see Gavin, but she knew she couldn't talk me out of it. She nibbled on her thumbnail before speaking.

"Are you sure about this?"

"Yes, I've waited long enough. I need to see him."

"Well, since you're already taking the risks, that little girl approached me again at the market today. I told her you'd be there tonight."

"Agnes?" I questioned, and Harp nodded. "I'll see what I can do for her." I looked out to the balcony as the last of the setting sun's rays shimmered through the arched glass doors. It would be dark enough soon to hide in the shadows. I walked over to my closet, walked in, and closed the door behind me, eyeing the box I hid the guard leathers I used to escape in. I opened it and pulled them out.

My heart sank as I remembered the last time I had left in them. Not for Gavin, but for the small child in tattered clothes in search of food and medicine for her family. The child who had to grow up long before her time. That night seemed so long ago now. The memories of it were bittersweet. The same night Agnes was trying her best to provide was the same night I had met a man who changed my life—my heart—forever.

I pulled myself out of my memories and dressed in my leathers. Walking out of the closet, I sensed Harper's worried eyes following me as I prepared for the night. Entering the bathroom, I wrapped the elixirs in cloth to keep them from clanking together in my pack before tossing it over my shoulder. Sheathing my dagger at my hip, I made my way out into my room where Harper was pacing in front of my bed. I walked over to her and pulled her into a tight hug before she could try to yell at me or tell me how crazy I was for trying to see Gavin. I pulled back to see her eyes glossy with tears.

"Harp, I'll be fine."

"I know, I know. I just don't want to watch you endure any more than you already have." Her voice cracked, and I pulled her back into me. This was the first time I had seen Harper get emotional. I had always viewed her as the strong one between us—the confident one. Always so sure of herself, tonight I saw how hesitant she was to let me leave.

"He truly cares for you, more than you know." Her admission caught me off guard. I smiled disbelievingly at her.

"And what makes you say that?"

"Intuition." She wiped her eyes and gave me a weak smile.

"Right, of course." I let out a soft laugh and rolled my eyes. "When I actually want you to let me in on the gossip, you decide to keep quiet" She snorted at my statement and pulled me back into one last hug.

"I'll let you figure that one out on your own," she spoke before giving me one last squeeze. Pulling away, I straightened myself, making my way toward the door. I looked back before I stepped out.

"I'll be back before sunrise. Will you wait for me?"

"Always."

The moon loomed high in the night sky as I made my way through the garden. The narrow passages along the garden's edge had grown, leaving an overgrowth to trek through. It had been so long since I had traveled this way that the path I had created for myself was almost nonexistent now.

Going in this direction was a risk. I did not know if they had fixed the gate after my first meeting with Gavin. I knew he never told Fredrick about me, but had he told him about the gate? After a few moments of nothing but the sounds of crickets and the soft crunch of footsteps against the path, I came across the tree that had kept my escape route hidden all this time. I lifted some of the low-hanging branches to find the bars still broken, and finches fluttered in my chest. Gavin believed in me—in my intentions before he even knew what they were.

I pulled away at some vines to get through the opening before making my way to the familiar drop off spot I'd used for months before Gavin barged into my life. I hid behind the trees, facing away from the gate, and waited. Sitting in the dark with my thoughts, my feelings got the better of me as I thought about everything I would say to Gavin once I saw him.

I played the argument in my head at least ten times. I thought about it so much it made me angry. How could he do this? Take a punishment that he knew could very well kill him. My father didn't care about his knights, or servers, or bloody hell, even the townspeople. I could have lost him, and the thought fueled the raging fire burning in my chest.

After waiting for long minutes that felt like an eternity, with my emotions boiling, I placed a few of the elixirs next to the tree trunk and just hoped Agnes would come and get them sometime through the night. Leaving without seeing her and asking how she and her family had been left a dull ache in my chest.

I hoped everyone was doing better, but I didn't have the time to wait. I had to get to the knights' quarters to see Gavin. Glancing back once more at the tree, I pushed forward, looking around at my surroundings before darting through the trees toward the stone building the knights stayed in. I told Gavin in a note yesterday I would come to see him tonight. He never responded to it, maybe because he didn't want me to risk it, but he knew me better than that.

I hastily darted around a few more trees until an arm wrapped around my waist, hauling me behind the closest tree. I let out a yelp from the contact. A hard chest pushed against my front, making my back slam against the tree. Gavin's gaze found mine.

"What are you doing?" he questioned with a whisper, but he was definitely yelling as quietly as he could.

"What am I doing? What did you do? Gavin, you could have been killed!" I murmured loudly back, hearing the emotions building in my voice. A lump formed in my throat as I took him in. His brow creased together, and a small gleam of sweat covered his forehead from pain. But I watched his features soften at my response.

"Myla—" He tried to speak, but I cut him off.

"No! Gavin, He could've killed you!" My chest ached as my emotions overflowed within me. "He could have taken you from me, because the only thing that man lives for is to inflict misery on those he detests!" I choked on my words. The sobs had begun. I tried to catch my breath as Gavin crushed me into his chest.

"He's taken everything from me!" I cried.

"Myla, I'm here..." My knees went weak, causing us both to slide down the tree. I sat there as he kneeled in front of me and cradled me in his arms.

"I was so scared," I whispered, taking in a deep breath of him to calm my nerves. I pulled away, cupping his cheek with one of my palms and running a thumb over his stubbled face. Following suit, he used both hands to pull me into a devastatingly needy kiss. He wrapped his hands into the hair at the nape of my neck to get better access as our tongues glided against each other's. As I ran my hands up his back, he swallowed my soft moan. He pulled away too soon, his breaths heaving, his expression pained.

"I'm sorry, your back" I scrambled around him to see the damage as I lifted his shirt. Most of the wounds were scabbed over but still inflamed. One, in particular, was more irritated than the others, and I assumed that was the one my hands scratched at.

"Here." I dug through my pack to find one elixir left and some cream. "This should help. Drink this." I handed it to him while I stroked the cream into his skin and felt his muscles tense under my touch. "Sorry."

"It's alright, better your hands than Roland's." I let out a soft laugh before growing serious again.

"Gavin, why did you do it?" I finished lathering his back with medication and sat back against the tree again to face him, waiting for his response. Meeting his gaze, I saw nothing but sincerity in his eyes.

"I'd do it a thousand times if it meant you weren't the one in pain anymore." Tears lined my eyes as I wrapped my arms around his neck to avoid his back. He nuzzled into the crook of my neck, wrapping his muscular arms around me. I reveled in the feel of him, his strength, his warmth. Multiple footsteps sounded through the distant trees, knocking us back into the now.

"You have to get back, Myla." He glanced around at our surroundings before meeting my eyes again. "I'll distract them."

"What—no..."

"It's fine." He stood hastily, helping me up with him and leaning me back against the tree, and placed another soft kiss on my lips. "Now go," he whispered as he darted around the tree and started a conversation with the knights walking by as I slipped away into the darkness of night.

Chapter Eleven

MYLA

I hardly did a thing as Harper whisked herself around my room, grabbing jewelry and makeup. Which I was happy about considering how sore I was from my training sets. Even after everything that happened with Gavin, I never stopped doing them. It had been two weeks since his lashings. He returned to his knight duties a few days ago. The last few nights we had spent staying up together and talking about our dreams while sharing glances, small touches of endearment, and endless kisses. He reminded me last night that he would still be my escort to the ball tonight, which brought me back to Harper tightening my dress's bodice.

She had already put me in the dress she chose for tonight, and from what I could see when I looked down, it was stunning. The dark-blue dress had sequins throughout the sweetheart neckline that filled the bodice until they dispersed into the flare of the dress. It had long, laced sleeves filled with beautiful, intricate designs to my wrists. Harper had my hair wrapped up in small individual rags. She wrapped it a few hours ago; she swore it gave the best curls. The dress exposed my chest and shoulders for the jewelry Harper was going through now. She kept placing the necklaces up to my chest then wrinkling her nose and moving to the next potential choice. She had been so focused that I'd just been sitting here, lost in my thoughts.

Was it crazy for me to think about asking Gavin if he would want to be something more?

I knew it would have to be kept a secret, but I'd rather we be together in secret than to never take the chance at all. Harper finally picked a bold diamond necklace with an entangled design of small stones with one big one in the center. It was beautiful, but definitely something out of my comfort zone. I normally wore less showy things. She draped it around my neck and clasped it easily before looping the matching earrings into my ears.

I never wanted to have my ears pierced, but after Harper and I had one of our sleepovers, and a few too many drinks, she convinced me to let her use a needle to pierce them, and I never looked back. We still got a good laugh about it here and there. Harper was getting ready to do my hair and makeup before I finally spoke.

"Let's move over to the balcony. It's a beautiful day, and I never got my walk this morning." She followed my lead and I sat on one of the wooden chairs facing the gardens, feeling my leg muscles bark for trying to sit down, while she put her seat almost directly in front of me. Harper pulled my face in her direction.

"Here, stay still, close your eyes." I did as she said, feeling the small bristled brush dust my face with makeup before she lined my eyes and undid the rags from my hair. After almost an hour, she told me she was finished, and I thanked the gods. My back was aching from sitting straight as a board for so long.

I stood, stretching my sore muscles, before walking to the full-length mirror in the bathing chamber. I didn't even recognize myself. Not in a bad way. Harper had done an amazing job. I felt like a princess for once. Not one that had been locked away her entire life, but one who was true royalty and got treated like it.

She did an earth tone smokey look on my eyes with a neutral pink on my lips that reminded me of the blush roses in the garden. I looked beautiful. I was beautiful, and I couldn't remember the last time I thought that about myself. I could feel the knot rising in my throat, but I quickly swallowed it down as Harper came up behind me, gripping my shoulders.

"Are you ready!? It's almost time to leave!" She shrilled with excitement. Harper was so excited about the ball, she showed up to my room already dressed to go. She turned to the mirror, touching up by powdering her nose before I had time to respond. She pulled me out of the bathroom and to the bed to put on my shoes, and I was terrified. They were heels. I was clumsy enough in flats and she wanted to put me on heels for tonight. I furrowed my brow, giving her a bewildering look, and she cackled at me. "Oh, come on, Myla. They aren't that bad."

"Have you seen those? You could kill a man with them."

"That's the best part." She gave me a wink, and I couldn't help my laugh.

"You better be lucky I love you and I'm a lady of my word because I wouldn't wear these otherwise." I sat on the bench at the end of my bed, defeated, and slipped my feet into the ridiculous shoes, knowing they were going to hate me later for wearing them. They were about three inches tall, but that was three inches too many for somebody as clumsy as me.

I stood and paced a few steps back and forth to get a good feel for them before we left for the royal ballroom. A knock on the door caught my attention, and Harper rushed to open it. My heart plummeted to my gut at the sight of Gavin. He was wearing his full set of armor but this one was definitely a royal set. He must have been wearing it just for tonight. The bright silver metal was polished perfectly, his gauntlets filled with detailed designs etched into the metal. The pauldron on his right shoulder was larger, with wispy designs running through it. As a dark blue cape draped over his other shoulder, it almost made me wonder if Harper found out what he would wear to match us for tonight.

"My lady." His voice was low and sultry. Heat pooled in my core at the sound of his voice alone. I took a step forward after admiring his attire.

"Sir Gavin." I accepted his outstretched arm and wrapped my arm around his as we began the walk to the ballroom. He looked forward but whispered to me as we walked side by side.

"You look absolutely stunning, Princess."

"You clean up well yourself, Sir Gavin." He gave me a wink and I swear my knees went wobbly, and not from the heels.

Harper walked a few paces in front of us, giving us privacy on the walk to the ballroom. I didn't know why I felt nervous, but I didn't want to look like an idiot gawking at him, so I stared at some paintings hanging on the walls as we walked down the stairwell of my tower. I focused on keeping the heels of my feet steady in my shoes. It had been so long since I'd worn anything like this. It was silent the whole walk other than the loud admiring stares Gavin and I kept giving to each other along the way. In the distance, I could see big, luxurious ball gowns of all shapes and sizes entering through the main door, but Harper always insisted on us making a grand entrance. Harper turned to Gavin.

"Go on in and wait for her at the bottom of the grand stairwell. We'll come down shortly after being announced." Gavin gave a nod of his head but held his burning stare with me a moment longer before walking through the main doors with all the other guests. "Gosh, just marry the man already. I can see you ripping each other's clothes off with looks alone."

"Harper, my gosh, could you speak any louder? The entrance is right there."

"Oh please, the royals have far more important things to discuss, like which cheeses on the snack table are the most exquisite." She pointed her nose in the air, making a disgusted face, mocking them, and I covered my mouth with my hand to hold in a laugh, but it didn't work very well. We sauntered down the long hall and took our next left, where the door to the grand stairwell was opened for any royals to be introduced to the crowd below. A servant at the top waited for each person to tell him how they would like to be introduced before walking out into the light at the top of the descending staircase. Harper put her hands on my shoulders, guiding me up the stairs, and I did my best to keep my feet steady on the gold-veined marble in heels. I took each step up, gripping my sweaty palms into my gown.

"My lady, how would you like to be introduced?" the servant asked.

"Princess Myla is fine, thank you." Harper tapped the man on the shoulder.

"No, introduce her as Princess Myla Elouise Blake of Baela."

"Really, Harp?" I gave her a side-eye, but she smiled at me.

"You are the Royal Princess of Baela. You deserve to be treated like it." She turned to the man. "I'm her royal servant Harper

Nash. Thank you, sir." The servant moved his hand forward, motioning me to go ahead before Harper as he announced us next.

"Princess Myla Elouise Blake, and her royal servant, Harper Nash." I heard a light applause as I slowly made my way to the top of the stairs and looked over the railing into the crowd. My eyes roamed the faces, looking for someone in particular, until they found those piercing eyes staring right at me. My shoulders relaxed and my hands loosened from my ballgown once I saw Gavin. He eased everything in me, making me feel okay again.

Royal social gatherings like this had never been my strong suit, given my upbringing. Speaking of upbringing, I noticed my father walking through the crowd toward the bottom of the stairs. Dressed in the utmost fashions, his tunic was a deep plum color filled with all the small golden details, down to the rings on his fingers. I could already feel my body going rigid.

He cleared the floor of people and looked up at me with a beaming fake smile with his arm outstretched, waiting for me to lock arms with him as we put on the show for everyone to see. I made it to the last step, placing my arm in his as we walked into the ballroom. I peered over my shoulder, glancing at Harper and Gavin walking behind us a few paces away. Anyone else in the room would think my father and I looked like a lovely father and daughter, two peas in a pod, but Harper and Gavin could see it. The discomfort. The hoax of the situation.

My father whisked me off to the dance floor as a faster paced song was playing, and I followed his steps as he pulled me closer to him.

"Harper did a great job, darling. You look lovely tonight." I kept my sights set over his shoulder as we twisted and stepped to the music, not making eye contact.

"She did, thank you." At the next spin, I walked off the ballroom dance floor and into the crowd toward Harper who was speaking to another familiar face: Roland, Gavin's friend, who had grown into one of mine. He gave me a small bow before speaking.

"Your Highness, a pleasure." I almost wanted to laugh at the formality. I was fighting on the battlefield with this man not too long ago. He was my shoulder to cry on during Gavin's punishment. I knew he was being proper with all of us being on public display.

"Myla, could you give us a moment? I love this song, and I'd love to dance with Sir Roland." Harper gave me a knowing look with a rosy face and raised eyebrows as she turned toward Roland with a smile, and I could tell she definitely wanted alone time with him.

"Of course," I said while returning her smile and heading off to find Gavin standing off to the side of the crowd watching the doors and his surroundings for any potential threats. I swore, sometimes I felt the man took his job too seriously, but it was admirable. I walked up to him, catching him off guard. "Sir Gavin."

"Princess," he said with a small bow of his head.

"Would you dance with me?" I asked.

He looked around a moment before responding,

"I don't dance, Your Highness."

"Oh, come on, what if I said please?" He gave me that side smile that always warmed my heart.

"Maybe another time."

"You promise?"

"I promise." He glanced around the room before gazing back up at me with those piercing eyes of his.

"You better. I'll hold you to it," I said while smiling at him, and he winked at me, making my smile grow as I looked down to my feet, trying to keep myself steady in ankle breaking heels.

"Go on, you'll miss the song," he said right when a cool voice spoke through the dancers.

"May I interrupt?" A man walked up from behind me, touching the small of my back, making me turn around.

"Prince Wyatt, uh—of course, I suppose." I tried not to stumble over my words as my lips pulled down into a slight frown. Wyatt Stagwhind, Prince of Credia. I had known him most of my life. Before the war, the royals would get together and have their fancy tea parties and gatherings, and we would always run into each other. All the girls in Baela or, well, anywhere had always swooned over him. I never understood why they did. Maybe it was his confidence.

He swaggered himself around any place as if he owned it himself. He always made me feel uncomfortable, even as a young girl. It seemed me being the only girl who didn't chase him hurt his ego, so he'd find me instead. I had not seen him since before the war, and now he was a grown man. He had short blonde hair, brown eyes. He was shorter than Gavin but still a little taller than me with a clean-shaven face and a smile from ear to ear as he pulled me to the floor to dance with me.

"How do you like my outfit, darling? I chose the finest silks for the occasion, just for you." He placed his hand on my lower back, lower than I was expecting him to go, and I recoiled, trying to regain more space between us.

"They look great, Wyatt. You chose well," I spoke half-heartedly. He smiled to himself before glancing down at my dress.

"As did you. Although, I feel you would look better in a brighter color, darling. The dark blue makes you look a little washed out." I looked up to him in surprise at his bold comment.

"Excuse me." I pulled away as the song ended.

"Of course, love. We will get your wardrobe all sorted out once you're in Credia."

"Credia? What are you talking about?"

"Your father didn't tell you?"

"Tell me what?" I questioned as my heart rate quickened.

"He promised me your hand, in exchange for my land," he said as if it were the happiest news I had ever heard in my life. My stomach churned. If he thought I looked pale before, I was sure it was getting worse the longer I stood there.

"I have to go..."

"Not a problem, I'll see you later tonight at the announcement, fiancée." He spoke with cheer as he straightened his clothes and turned to walk away. I saw my father in the distance, sitting at his throne and watching the party unfold with Queen Lilith of Mayri next to him, talking about something. She was standing over his right shoulder with one arm draped over him, whispering in his ear with a seductive smile on her face. I tried to keep my walking steady in my heels even though I felt faint.

"Excuse me, Father, could I have a word?" He nodded to Lilith in dismissal before standing and walking arm and arm with me.

"Yes, darling?"

"Why would you promise my hand?"

"Because it was what Prince Wyatt wanted in exchange for what I wanted. It was business. You should be thanking me. He's royal, rich, and will take care of your needs."

"But I don't love him."

"Love won't get you anywhere in this world, Myla. The quicker you learn that, the better.

We will announce your engagement later tonight. Enjoy it." I felt the lump rising in my throat, but I forced myself to speak.

"Father, may I go out for a walk in the gardens?"

"Only because you asked nicely." He looked at me with a side-eye before releasing my arm. "Don't forget to take an escort with you and be back for the announcement." He waved his hand as he walked back to his throne.

"Thank you," came out barely above a whisper before I rushed toward the doors. I needed air. I couldn't breathe. The walls felt like they were caving in around me as I hurried down the long halls, trying to find my way out of this place. Out of this nightmare. Out of this life. I heard shuffling footsteps behind me, but I kept moving forward. Where were the gardens? I tripped over my feet and fell to my knees. When I looked up, Harper and Gavin were in front of me on the ground, too, with concerned expressions.

"Did he hurt you?" And I couldn't keep the tears in a moment longer as they fell from my eyes at Gavin's question. Harper pulled me into her embrace, trying to calm my silent sobs. After a few moments, I collected myself and Gavin helped me to my feet.

"I just want to take a walk in the garden." I spoke with a numb calm before looking at Harper.

"I'll let you two go. It'll give you time alone," she said, giving me a soft smile and another hug. "Let me know if you want me to go back to your room after the ball. I can sneak out with all the food and a bottle of wine. Nobody ever needs to know." She gave me a wink, trying to ease me.

"Yes on the bottle of wine." I gave a forced smile before she walked off, and it was just Gavin and me. I wasn't sure if I ran or walked out of the ballroom in my panic, but at the end of the hall was the garden foyer. Gavin walked next to me quietly, offering me the comfort of his presence as we walked out through the foyer, and the smell of the wildflowers and roses calmed my racing thoughts.

"Wait a second." Gavin stopped next to me from my words as I rested my hand on his shoulder, using him to help me keep my balance as I slipped my shoes off, one after the other. "Much better." He shook his head with a smile.

"Why did you wear those if you hate them so much?"

"I promised Harper she could pick out my clothes for tonight, and she chose to torture my toes." He let out a full, genuine laugh, and it was like the world melted away. He looked back at me again.

"Would you like to tell me what happened back there?" He raised a brow, and I interlocked my arm around his.

"Walk with me. I'll tell you once we're there."

"Lead the way, Myla." Gavin saying my name instead of some formal title caught me off guard considering we were still in public, but we were alone in the garden, so I guessed that reasoning behind it sufficed. We walked through the narrow paths and down one of the tall, hedged hallways before making it to one of my favorite places in the garden: the fountain.

My mother and I came here a lot when I was young, but as I had gotten older, I quit coming as often as I used to. Considering I might not see it for much longer if I'd be moving to Credia, I couldn't think of anyone else I'd rather be out here with.

I ran my fingertips along the smooth stone before sitting on the fountain ledge. Setting my heels on the ground next to me,

I admired the three tiers laced with designs etched in the stone, creating little passageways for the water to travel down to each tier. I could hear the soothing sound it made as it rippled into the biggest pool of water at the bottom.

The cool autumn air made the fabric of my dress flow with the wind. A chill crept over my skin. Gavin took the cape attached to his armor off and draped it over my shoulders.

"Question for a question," I said, looking at the water as the small coins lying at the bottom of the fountain reflected off the moonlight.

"By all means." I could feel his stare, but I was too scared to look at him without completely falling apart again.

"What would you do if the one thing you thought you had control over was ripped away from you? Would you try to chase what you wanted and suffer the consequences, or would you do as you're told?"

He moved to sit next to me, turning toward me so I would look at him. Glancing down, he hummed in contemplation to himself before looking at me again. His soft smile wavered before he responded.

"Depends on what the one thing is?"

"Marriage... I always thought I would marry for love, not out of duty for someone else's desires. I guess that was a naïve dream." He placed his hand over mine on the smooth stone fountain.

"I would do whatever would bring me happiness."

"Neither brings me happiness, this castle or this marriage. What I truly want I can't have." I built up the courage to meet his moonlit eyes, his face somehow inches from mine now. I felt the warmth of his breath against my neck when he spoke again.

"What is it you truly want, Myla?" I gazed from his lips and then back to his eyes as my breath hitched in my chest.

"You." My voice cracked against the rock of emotions in my throat as I tried to hold myself together. His palms cupped my face, pulling me into a heated kiss before I could catch my breath. His hands moved to my waist, pulling me onto his lap without breaking our connection. I ran my fingers through his hair, pulling him deeper into our kiss, opening my mouth further to give us both more access. His calloused hands gripped my thighs under my dress.

A whimper of pleasure escaped me. Bringing his hands back to my waist, he pulled me against his cold metal armor, sending a shiver up my spine. Pulling away, he placed his forehead against mine as we both caught our breath. He furrowed his brow and looked at me with tear-lined eyes. I already knew what was about to say, and I couldn't stop the tears that started leaking from my eyes.

"Gavin, please."

"Myla... we can't keep doing this. Your father would do unspeakable things if he found out and I—" He shook his head, looking away from me, his eyes glossy with tears. "I can't live with that."

"Can't live with what?" I murmured.

"Live in a world without you in it because of me... At least this way you still get to live; you still get to have a life."

"I don't want to live a life without you in it," I spoke without a doubt in my mind about what I felt for this man. He wiped away the last of the tears falling from my eyes, never meeting them.

"Myla—" I cut him off.

"Then don't promise me forever, Gavin." I palmed his cheek, pulling his face to mine again. "Promise me the time we have left." He finally looked me in the eye. "Promise me we'll make the best of it." He finally gave me that side smile that always made my knees weak.

"Okay... I promise to make the best of the little time we have left together." My lips curved into a smile as I moved off his lap so he could stand. He offered me his hand to finish our walk in the gardens.

"Wait, I wanted to do one last thing with you before we go. Do you have two coppers?" He reached into one of his pockets and pulled out the coins and I took one. "I want us to make a wish at the fountain. My mother and I would always make a wish when we stopped here. She told me stories about how they would come true."

"She sounds like a lovely woman," he spoke with a warm expression. We both sat, turning our backs to the fountain, and tossed the coins over our shoulders to make a wish.

"So, what did you wish for?" he asked.

"Well, I can't tell you because then it will not come to be!" We both huffed a laugh, taking one last look at the fountain, trying to see which coin was the one we tossed in.

"Well, I wished for a cold bath," he joked in a soft, husky tone. Tilting his head to the side, he gave me a teasing smile about his arousal. Heat flushed my cheeks as I bit my lip, and when I put my hand down on the fountain's ledge to push myself back onto my bare feet, my hand completely missed the ledge and I fell into the fountain. The chilled water soaked into my dress, and my skin pebbled as the cool air blew through the garden.

"Myla! Are you alright?" Gavin held out his hand, and I grabbed it, yanking him into the fountain with me. Water splashed over the edges of the gray stone, and the water from the fountain's tier flowed over Gavin's head while he looked at me with narrowed eyes.

"Your wish is my command," I said, grinning at him. We both burst out in laughter in the pool of water, surrounded by the wishes of those before us.

Chapter Twelve

MYLA

The walk back to my room tower to get changed was bittersweet. We both knew we couldn't continue our romantic endeavors, but I knew we also were going to make the best of the time we had left together. Whatever that entailed was yet to be determined. Gavin told me he would keep his word and still come to my room every morning to practice and would teach me new moves every couple of days. To learn how to better defend myself.

I was already feeling more confident with the few small things he had shown me. Gavin waited by the door as I walked into my room. I didn't have time to fix myself back up again. Luckily, the dress took the most damage instead of me, but the ends of my hair were damp after being dipped in the fountain. I quickly changed into a simpler dress and put on some flats that were more comfortable than those heels. I walked back out into the hall with a sigh at how much better my feet felt walking on flat ground. Gavin noticed the gesture and let out a laugh to himself.

"What? You would feel the same if—" But my thought got cut off by the roaring cheers from the ballroom. The announcement. The engagement. Oh god! Gavin took notice of the panicked look on my face because we quickly started running to the ballroom, down the spiral stairs, through all the long hallways. Before we could make it there, I got yanked to a side room by the icy hands of my father.

My eyes adjusted to the light of the room right when Gavin turned the corner and became still as stone when he saw my father standing there, along with Prince Wyatt. Wyatt was leaning against the small table in the room, admiring his reflection in the silverware and fixing his tousled hair, unfazed by what was happening around him until my father cleared his throat and glared at him. He put down the spoon and spoke.

"Myla, it broke my heart when you didn't show up to the engagement announcement. Not only did you miss our announcement, but you also missed your father's." He looked at me with insincere eyes, and a part of me felt like Wyatt didn't have a genuine bone in his body.

Everything he did or said, he acted out perfectly to fit his egotistical view of himself. "What announcement?" I looked at my father, who had gone silent in his anger.

"I am to be married to Queen Lilith of Mayri, but you would know that if you would have shown up to begin with." Pain bloomed across my cheek as he backhanded me, and Gavin rushed to my side.

"Leave her." My father spoke sternly, with eyes filled with fury. Gavin turned his head away, knowing it would incline my father to kill him where he stood if he didn't obey. King Henry continued. "Everything is finally coming together. Eventually all the lands will become the Kingdom of Baela and I will rule it all with Lilith by my side." I looked at Prince Wyatt.

"And you're okay with this? Losing your land, your kingdom, your throne. For what? My hand?" I questioned, anger lacing my tone.

"Your father and I have an understanding," Wyatt spoke calmly. "I will continue to keep things in order for your father, our king, in Credia, while he rules the kingdoms from Baela."

"What more are you getting out of this? No man gives up power for nothing." My father stepped forward.

"Wyatt gets the throne when I die, but until then he remains loyal to me. He still gets to run things in Credia under my command, while keeping all his father's riches and royalty..." Henry stepped forward, his breath reeking of whiskey as he cupped my cheek. I turned my face away from him. "...that he can shower his new bride with if he so wishes." His whisper crept over my skin, making it crawl as he rubbed his thumb over my now bruised cheek. I brought my eyes back to my father fearlessly.

"I don't care about riches and royalty," I spat, and he pulled his hand back again, but Gavin grabbed his wrist.

"Your Majesty, I understand you're upset, but it is still my duty to protect the Princess." He released my father's wrist and took a step back, and I had never felt more in awe of him. The gesture might have been small to him, but I had never had someone stop my father from laying a hand on me. My father stepped toward Gavin, standing toe to toe with him before Wyatt came forward, intervening. He placed a steady hand on both of their shoulders.

"The knight has a point. When you promised your daughter to me for my lands, she officially became my property, and I'd like her to remain..." Wyatt paused, stepping away from Gavin and the wicked King of Baela, walking the few short steps to me he clasped my chin between his fingers, bringing his nose down my collarbone and inhaling my scent. "...untouched." He finished his statement while turning my face back to his. The man tried to kiss me. I jerked my head away, making him kiss my sore cheek instead.

"Hmm, want to wait, do you? That's fine because I'll have you all to myself soon enough." He released my face and started toward the door. I was disgusted by his touch alone. The bile rose in my throat, causing a burn in my chest.

"I must get back to Credia before my father tries to send any more traders to your gates."

"The attack on the gate was Credia?" I turned to him with narrow eyes.

"Yes, dear, I'm afraid it was. My father is close to his deathbed, but he still has those who loyally follow his orders, like those poor souls that tried to attack your castle that day. They were coming for you, darling." He moved his hands together, making them look like a steeple before pressing them to his lips and then pointing it towards me. "My father thought he could eliminate the one thing I've wanted since I was a boy then make me take the throne and become king once he's dead." He rolled his eyes. "But why do that when I can relax now and in the future rule everything?" He looked back at me with his eyes going more serious. "I'm going to enjoy my days as a prince with my bride by my side."

"You don't even know me," I spat, feeling the anger rising in me.

"True, I know little. We'd know plenty about one another if you would have written back all those years. But we will get to know each other, Myla. We have the rest of our lives and I'm already so captivated by you." Bile rose in my throat again as I started fiddling with the diamonds around my neck. I tried to come up with something to say to this psychotic person in front of me. I came up empty. How could you love someone you hardly knew?

I asked myself that question, and yet, I had always felt a connection with Gavin. From the moment I met him, there was this attraction. With Wyatt, that attraction was never there. I hadn't seen or been around Wyatt in years, then he showed up out of the blue asking my father for my hand. I didn't even like him when we were younger, regardless of what all the other girls thought about him. What made him so confident that I'd fall in love with him now when he was even more smug than he was back then?

I thought I was going to be sick. His scent reeked of tobacco. I rubbed my hands down my face, trying to rub the lingering smell away. I tried to hide my shudder while I took in everything I had heard as Wyatt walked toward the door.

"I'll see you before winter's end, my dear," he called over his shoulder toward me before turning to my father. "Be sure she arrives on time for that, at least," he said prior to bumping into Gavin's shoulder on his way out, giving him the snarl all the royals gave to the servants or anyone who they considered "lesser than." My father looked lost in violent thought as he turned to Gavin and me.

"You're dismissed," he said, twisting the gold ring on his pinky finger. A tick. "You should be happy. If it weren't for your prince, I'd be having Fredrick escort you to my office." He gave me a small smile filled with venom before I walked out of the room, but he stopped Gavin from leaving and slammed the door in my face. I paced outside the door. Panic rose in my chest, making every muscle tighten.

Chapter Thirteen

GAVIN

"Would you like a drink?" King Henry asked as he walked back behind his desk, pulling out a glass bottle full of amber liquid and two glasses.

"No, thank you, Your Majesty" was all I said as the silence stretched between us, the only sound being the liquor pouring into his glass. He picked it up, taking a long sip before he spoke again.

"Sit," he said firmly, and I obliged. "Your Majesty—"

"Shut up," he spoke in a cool calm. My hands clenched, and my jaw pulsed as I tried to keep my calm against a man I had lost all respect for.

"Do you think I'm stupid, Sir Gavin?"

"No, Your Majesty." I never met his dark gaze.

"Do you think I don't know about this attraction between yourself and my daughter?" I met his eyes at his words, but I had nothing to say because I knew it to be true. I couldn't deny that I had a pull—a weakness for Myla.

"Ah, that got your attention, didn't it?" He smirked at his attentiveness before his face fell more serious. "I'm going to need you to listen closely, Sir Gavin," he spat out his words threateningly while interlocking his gold cuffed fingers and leaned back in his chair. "You and a small group of men will escort my daughter to Credia, not because I like you, but because I can't wait to hear all about the knight that had to hand over the woman he loved." He paused for a moment as if he wanted to get a rise out of me, but I wouldn't give him the satisfaction of my broken heart. This man indulged in others' pain. Emotional or physical didn't matter. He wanted Myla and I to suffer however he could deliver it, satiating his need to cause more damage.

"This allure you both have needs to stop. From this moment forward, you will be her knight and nothing more. If I find out that your draw to one another impedes my plans, I'll do unspeakable things to you both myself, and then I'll pay a visit to a woman named Beth in your regard." His words caused me to jolt to my feet in anger, gripping the hilt of my sword.

"Watch it, sir, wouldn't want you to make any hasty decisions." He stood, making sure his threat had been delivered before dismissing me with a nod of his head towards the door. "Oh, and Gavin, keep this between us. We wouldn't want Myla to understand why her knight turned away from her now, would we?" He grinned as his words twisted a knife in my chest. He wanted me to break Myla's heart further for his sick fixation on others' misery. I spoke no other words as he walked around his desk and opened the door.

Chapter Fourteen

MYLA

The door opened and Gavin looked at me, but I couldn't discern the emotion in his eyes.

"Goodnight," my father spoke without looking back toward us again. He walked in the direction of the King's quarters while Gavin returned me to my prison tower of a room without a word. It was the first time he ever walked three paces in front of me. Every step staring at his back shoved the stake further into my hollow, bleeding heart.

The days turned into weeks, going by in a blur. I couldn't believe I would leave for Credia tomorrow, promised to be married to Prince Wyatt. The snobbiest royal of all. The last time I saw him was during that meeting with my father after the engagement announcement, where I caught him admiring his own reflection in the leftover dinner silverware from the ball.

Gavin had been distant ever since he got locked in that room with my father. He had remained distant even though I tried to talk to him about it. I hated Wyatt, but what was I to do? I had always been a prisoner. Chained to whatever future my father would gain from. Every choice or action made for me was done by him just so he could get a step closer to his desires.

I dreamt of one day being able to make my own choices. I'd do it all, everything, without anything or anyone getting in my way. Maybe if I stayed tucked away in my bed and forgot about what I'd been told to do, the world around me would disappear.

I could picture what my life would be like with Gavin: looking into his eyes every morning, living in his small hometown, taking morning walks on the sandy beaches hand in hand, reminiscing about how far we had come. I wished that were my reality, but Gavin had barely talked to me since he spoke with my father for those few moments. I didn't know what the King said, but based on Gavin trying to be brief all the time, I assumed it was something bad. A warning.

A knock on the door disturbed my train of thought. I didn't bother getting out of bed. I already knew it was Gavin. *Speak of the devil.*

He was here for our morning training session. For the last few weeks, it had taken everything in me to keep my distance and desires for this man at bay. He kept his word. He came to my room every morning for our training session together before heading off to the knights' quarters to get a rest in before the next night shift. I hadn't felt his lips or hands on me since our encounter at the fountain, and I'd be lying if I said I didn't miss his touch. The taste of him. What his hair felt like threaded through my fingers.

How we were going to spend three days traveling to Credia together, I didn't know. Regardless of the other knights being there or not, it would be the freest I had ever been in my entire life. I didn't know if I'd have enough self-control with Sir Gavin Dawson guarding me for three days, mostly alone in the wilderness between here and the next kingdom. Gavin walked through the door and I could feel the blush heating my cheeks because of where I had let my thoughts wander to.

He had been distant ever since the encounter with my father. Careful not to get too close. He even kept our conversations shorter, straightforward, and more to the point. I understood. I was promised to be married to another man, but it didn't make the distance between us hurt any less. Before everything turned into a mess, I took it for granted. I missed our talks, smiles, laughs, his caresses, and his fervent kisses.

Gavin set down a heavy bag that thudded against the floor, and I looked down at it, confused, before bringing my eyes back to his.

"What's this?"

"A gift"

"For?" I asked with a smile slowly pulling up at my lips.

"You've been doing well with your training lately so I wanted to get you something for all of your hard work." He looked out toward the sunrise through the balcony door windows, breaking our gaze. "And this will be our last session together before our journey to Credia for your upcoming wedding, so think of it as a parting gift."

My smile wavered at that while I got out of bed to open the large bag. I pulled out high quality fighting leathers with a sheathed sword, but not just any sword. This one was a custom. It was shorter than Gavin's and lighter, making it easier to wield. They wrapped the handle with sturdy black leather, while the pommel at the end of the handle had an elegant bluestone twisted within the metal. It was beautiful and more than just a sword to me. It represented me and who I was becoming. I wasn't some weak damsel that couldn't handle her own.

A part of me felt empowered to start fresh in Credia as someone who could stand her ground against whatever came my way. Someone who could stand taller, brighter. Someone who wasn't afraid. Although I wanted to be all of those things, the thought of not being able to do them with Gavin brought tears to my eyes. He had been my inspiration from the moment I met him.

He made me feel something again after the years of living in my father's shadows. After being bloodied and beaten, he was there to heal my wounds, and I could never thank him enough for that. I didn't deserve these gifts. I should have been getting him something. He moved next to me with concern filling his stare as I looked up at him.

"Is something wrong? They should fit you well. Harper told me what size to purchase." And at that, my tears streamed faster at the effort that went into the gift.

"Nothing's wrong. It's perfect, beautiful, really. You shouldn't have. If anything, I should be giving you a gift."

"I assure you, you've given me more than enough, Princess." He held my gaze with his admission. I swiped my tears away hastily before he looked away again, clearing his throat while getting back to his feet. "Go try them on, and then we can have our session." I walked to the bathing chamber dumbfounded on what to say to this man that I'd fallen for but could not have, knowing that after our journey to Credia, we would have to say our goodbyes and walk away. I wasn't ready. I didn't think I'd ever be.

Chapter Fifteen

Gavin

Watching her during our last training session wearing the fighting leathers, wielding a sword of her own made her look as if she were glowing. Proud even, to do something more to defend herself. My heart swelled in my chest at the sight of her growth, her confidence. For the last couple of weeks, trying to maintain my distance from her had been more challenging than being at war. But what choice did I have?

Her father gave me a warning. If I didn't stop pursuing Myla, he would punish us both. I wasn't worried about myself. Couldn't care less about what that coward of a man would try to do to me. I cared about what would happen to my family, to Myla. Her well-being was all that mattered to me now. Although I didn't want her to marry another man, Wyatt didn't seem like the type to abuse her like her own father had, and that brought me some relief.

I wanted to live in a world where she was alive and well, where I knew she was safe, even if it wasn't within my arms. No matter how hard my heart desired to be with her, I had accepted she would never be mine.

She finished the exercises for the morning right when Harper busted open the door and saw her wearing the leathers and sword. Her eyes went wide.

"You look like a warrior!" She rushed to Myla, giving her a big warm hug before pulling away. "Good thing you came to me, Gavin." She looked Myla up and down before looking at me. "They definitely flatter your figure." She gave me a wink, and a smile tugged up at my lips.

Harper had been a great friend to Myla. I hoped she had decided to go with her to Credia, but I knew Myla would never ask that of her. I wanted Myla to have something familiar, something constant in her life while living in a new kingdom. If Harper stayed in Baela, at least Myla would have the sword and leathers to remind her of our time together.

"I'll leave you two to it then." I gave them both a nod of farewell but Myla's voice stopped me.

"Gavin." I turned to look at her. Those deep blue eyes filled with storms of emotions. I saw all of them the fear, the uncertainty. Everything she never said, she said with those eyes. I saw it because I felt it too, so I reassured her, even though I knew the end would come sooner than either of us ever wanted it to.

"No goodbyes today. I'll see you in the morning by the gate. We leave at sunrise with Roland and the others." I noticed Harper look to her feet at the mention of Roland, and it made me wonder what he had been up to here recently since he hadn't been in my business like he normally was. I turned toward the door, feeling Myla watching my every step until her bedroom door shifted behind me. It was as if I had shoved all of my feelings in that room and locked the door while someone else held the key.

After leaving Myla's room, I walked over to the knights' quarters looking for Roland. The last few weeks, we had hardly seen each other between shifts and eating together in the mess hall. Now that I thought about it, that was probably where he was to begin with.

I changed course to the mess hall, and it didn't take me long to get there. When I spotted Roland, he had already bathed from the overnight shift. His black hair was still wet, pulled back at the nape of his neck. He was wearing his casual clothes but still had his sword strapped to his hip. Maybe it was a knight thing or the fear of being without it, but I didn't think either of us had ever gone anywhere without our swords since the war ended.

It was like it had become an extension of who we both were. He waved me over, and I walked around the tables filled with morning chatter. Walking over to his table, I sat in front of him. Pulling out a flask from one of his pockets, the metal still shining from being polished, with the royal crest designs engraved along the front of it, he slid it to me, and I looked at him, surprise etched in my features.

"What? I told you I wanted to go out for drinks soon. I figured now is as good as ever since we will transport the love of your life to another man tomorrow," Roland said, and I rolled my eyes at his blunt statement, taking a long swig from the flask, feeling the heat slide down my throat, settling deep in my gut, making my whole core heat. Whatever was in the flask was definitely something strong, as I almost coughed, trying to catch my breath from the clear liquor.

"How did you know about tomorrow? I haven't said anything, and you usually get your information from me." Looking at him with a smirk, I had a good idea of whom he had been conversing with.

"I have just been listening to the kingdom gossip, is all." He took a swig from the flask.

"Or maybe you've been getting all your gossip from a certain redhead," I said, and he looked down at his hands clasped around his flask before looking at me with a gloating smile on his face that told me everything I already knew.

"You've been seeing Harper, haven't you? Mr. Stay away from the Princess and then you go for her servant."

"Hey, that's not fair. Harper is still a servant. At least I can actually be with her." His words cut deep and I watched the expression change on his face. "Gavin, I'm sorry. I didn't mean for it to come out that way."

"It's alright. You're not wrong, no matter how much I want you to be." I raked my hands over my face before grabbing the flask and taking another long swig. I was already feeling my thoughts and surroundings slow down from the alcohol, and the aches in my chest weren't as strong as they were when I left Myla's room. "Tell me about you and Harp. Is it serious?"

"She's everything I've ever wanted and more. I never thought I could love somebody like this."

"Love? How long have you guys been talking?"

"We started talking when we exchanged the notes between you and Myla, and then the night of the ball when her date, some moron named Tomas, stood her up, we danced all night, and I haven't stopped talking to her since. I fell for her that night."

"I'm happy for you, brother," I said while taking another considerable drink.

"Thank you." He looked at me with an apologetic smile but I could tell he was holding something back from me. I slid the flask back to him.

"Roland, what aren't you telling me?" He looked back at me, taking another long swig from the flask before letting out a shaky breath.

"I'll always be there for you, you know that—" I cut him off.

"Cut the sap, friend, and get to the point."

"I put in a request for resignation a few days ago, and this morning, they approved it. The mission to transport Myla will be my last. I'm going wherever Harper goes." His hands fiddled with the flask nervously but I wasn't mad. I truly was happy for him. My wide grin caught him off guard, but I stood reaching across the table to give him a quick one-armed hug with a few heavy pats on his back.

"Why would you think I'd be mad? Roland, you deserve to go home, to be happy, and start a life outside of all the kingdom shit we've had to deal with. I truly am happy for you." I sat back down and I could see Roland's shoulders sag in relief. His news had been weighing on his mind.

"But what about you?" he questioned, his eyes going soft.

"I think that means I'll need more of this," I said, grabbing the empty flask from his hand again. He laughed as I went for a refill. Then we sat and chatted about all his plans for the future.

A part of me felt empty, while my intoxicated mind wandered. I had always been a man of my word, but that night at the ball I never danced with Myla even though I told her I would another time, and now I didn't know if that time would ever come. Roland and I finished the flask more than once before I staggered to the knight's quarters to get some sleep.

My demons haunted my dreams.

Chapter Sixteen

Gavin

My head pounded as the morning light shined through the canopy of trees overhead. I waited for Myla at the back gate before we began our travels to Credia. I couldn't remember the last time Roland and I had drinks. Personally, I didn't drink very often, but with what was happening, Roland figured I could use it, and I didn't disagree with him.

Roland checked the straps on the horses and carriage while we waited. King Henry didn't want a crowd on guard for our trip. He said the less noticed we were, the better since the current King of

Credia wanted Myla's head on a platter. King Ferand wanted the deal between Prince Wyatt and King Henry to fall through.

The cool, crisp morning air helped to wake me up some, considering the last couple of weeks I hadn't been getting much sleep. If it wasn't the nightmares of war keeping me up, it was the thoughts of Myla running through my head. Our last kiss was everything. I didn't know how much longer I could control the urges to stay away from her.

I had been doing my best: keeping the conversations short during our training, not getting too close to her, but I couldn't stop myself when she started shedding tears. I wanted to hold her close and wipe them away, but the smallest of touches between us always sent a shock through my veins. The carriage was facing the wooded path as I leaned up against it. The frost from the wintry nights had already melted, causing the ground to be a little muddy, but nothing the carriage shouldn't be able to make it through.

I turned to peer back at the castle, seeing Myla standing just a few yards away, carrying two small bags. She wasn't beaming like she normally was, but how could I blame her? The King had decided every choice throughout her whole life for her. Even down to the man she was supposed to marry. A man she should love. A man like me, but I refused to let my mind linger on those impossibilities.

I stepped forward, grabbed her bags, and put them in the back of the carriage. Myla said nothing to me, but her eyes showed me everything I needed to see. She was scared, hurt, and tired, and it killed me. I just wanted to take her away in this carriage and live out the rest of our lives together, but we'd have to run from everything, and that wasn't a way to live. Besides, if I didn't continue making money, I wouldn't be able to send anything to my mother each month to keep the farm running and my siblings taken care of. But how far was a man willing to go for someone he believed was the love of his life? Would my family understand?

What was duty and honor if the one thing you wanted to be fighting for wasn't around anymore? A squeal from behind me pulled my head in that direction and I saw Harper running through the garden towards the carriage, arms full of everything but the kitchen sink. When I glanced over at Myla, she was smiling again, and it made everything else in my mind fade away.

Roland jogged past me as Harper dropped all of her things and jumped into his arms. He gave her a quick spin and a passionate kiss before putting her down while Myla and I watched. I did my best to not make eye contact with her when she peered at me with that same fire in her eyes that Roland and Harper had. I had to remind myself why I was doing this: to keep her safe from her father and his punishments and from Wyatt. What would he do to her if he found out about some of our heated encounters?

Seeing how obsessed he was with her, I was assuming it wouldn't be anything good. Roland placed Harper back on the ground, holding her for a few moments before finally letting her go. He helped her with her things as they walked the rest of the way to the carriage. Harper threw her stuff in the back, making the back wheels of the carriage sink into the moist ground at how heavy it was.

"Jeez, Harp, what did you bring?" Myla asked.

"Oh, you know, just the essentials," she responded with a wide smile before wrapping her arms around Myla. "I hope you didn't think you could get rid of me by leaving to another kingdom in the early hours of the morning." Harper gave her a side-eye.

"No, I didn't think you would want to come with me. I'm sure I'll have another royal servant in Credia. I couldn't ask you to pack up your life and leave Baela. This is your home just as much as it is—" Myla paused, looking down. "—was my home." Myla glanced back to Harper. "I know I was more of a royal prisoner of Baela, but this place was still my home. I was born here, and it's the only place I have ever made memories." Harper grabbed Myla's hand.

"Well, that means we have a lot of new memories to make." Harper gave Myla another smile before opening the carriage door for them both to climb inside. Roland hopped in the carriage box seat, readying to go, while I got on top of my horse in one swift motion. I looked over to the carriage, seeing Myla looking at me through the small round window, and I did my best to give her a reassuring smile, but we both recognized the truth behind this trip. These would be the last few days we would get together, and I wasn't sure how to make the best of it while also keeping my emotions in check.

Six more knights rode through the castle gate before it closed behind them. Two hurried to the front, while two stayed toward the back, and the last two trotted to either side of the carriage. I nudged my horse forward, glancing over to her one last time, right when Roland called me over to him, handing me the map with two paths marked for our journey.

"Which do you want to take? We can take the northern mountain pass, but it'll add more time to our trip. I didn't think you would want to take the eastern route because—"

"The mountain pass." I cut him off before he could finish, and he looked down for a moment with a concerned expression on his face before setting the map down and looking forward, making a clicking sound with his mouth to get the horse moving along the trail. I followed next to the carriage without another word.

By nightfall, we found a spot to camp for the night. There was a small clearing in the thick woods, just enough room for the carriage, to tie up the horses, lay out our bedrolls, and have a fire. The seasons were quickly changing from autumn to winter. The nights were becoming crisp, while the days were cooling down. Tomorrow we should start the day early to take advantage of the weather on our longer journey taking the pass, but for now, we really needed to rest the horses and get some sleep.

Sleep. I didn't think I had had a restful night of sleep since that night in Myla's room. Not one nightmare entered my mind with her in my arms. I shook away the thought while getting off my horse and began helping Roland set up camp.

"I'll go find firewood," Roland spoke to me before walking off into the woods right when Harper sauntered out of the carriage.

"Myla fell asleep. Is there anything I can help with?"

"Yeah, could you grab the bedrolls out of the carriage?"

"No problem." She walked to the back of the carriage while I unhooked the horses, giving them a break from the load. I tied a bag of oats to the tree nearby so they could both get something to eat. I walked to the door of the carriage while Harper finished setting up the bedrolls. Myla had her arm up against the wall of the carriage, asleep, using it as a pillow.

"Has she been okay?" I asked Harper without taking my eyes off of Myla.

"She hasn't been sleeping much, I think she's excited to see more than just the castle and the same old garden, but I know she doesn't want to experience those things with Prince Wyatt." Glancing over my shoulder at her, she gave me a narrowed expression before rolling her eyes at me. "Why are men so dense sometimes?" she asked herself.

"Did you just call me stupid?"

"Respectfully, yes." I furrowed my brow at her. "Tell her how you feel."

"I can't."

"Why can't you?"

"Because it's not that easy for us like it is for you and Roland. You two can be together. She's a princess, and I'll never be able to give her a royal life, nor would she be able to be with someone who isn't royalty. This trip makes that obvious."

"If you think Myla cares anything about royal life, then you don't know her at all, and who cares if she's the Princess of Baela. When you love something, you climb over the walls to get it."

"You don't understand, Harp. Her father would kill both of us if he caught us, and who knows what Wyatt would do? I can't risk her safety over my feelings for her."

"What about her happiness? Her feelings? Why don't you ask her what she truly wants before assuming that she wouldn't risk it all, including her safety, for the freedom to make her own choice?" The frustration rose in me, but I did my best to keep my voice down.

"Really? Has she told you what she truly wants? Has she told you what she'd be willing to risk over her freedom and safety?" She rushed over to me, looking up to me to meet my eyes, practically nose to nose.

"No, she hasn't, but I've known and been around Myla my entire life, and it's not that hard to see it, Gavin." We both jolted toward the sound of twigs snapping to our right, seeing Roland walk through the trees, looking at us.

"What did I miss?" He gaped at us standing feet apart from each other with narrowed eyes, and the tension slowly eased from the air.

"Nothing, just a chat, darling," Harper spoke up while walking over to Roland, helping him with some of the firewood. Roland's eyes darted between the two of us. He looked at me in question, as if he were asking me what happened with a glance alone. I shook my head, and he turned to camp, wood in hand to get the fire started for the night. I turned towards the carriage. Myla was still sleeping.

Gosh, had we both been unable to sleep these last couple of weeks? Did I wreck her dreams at night like she did mine? I scooped one arm under her knees while placing the other under her arms and lifted her effortlessly into my arms, resting her head against my chest. But in the first few steps to camp, she jolted awake.

"Hey, it's okay. I got you," I murmured, and she relaxed in my arms, holding my stare a moment too long before placing her head back against my chest. It was almost as if she were reveling in the feel of me holding her as much as I was. I held her tightly and even slowed my walk a little because I knew as soon as we got to the campsite a few more paces ahead, I'd have to return to reality.

Her scent engulfed me—sweet wildflowers. It had been weeks since I had held her in my arms, weeks since I had taken in a deep breath of her. I placed her feet on the ground but her hand lingered on my chest before she moved it back to her side. She went to sit next to Harper who once again rolled her eyes at me like I was a complete idiot. I bent down to get the fire started while Roland rolled over an oversized log and used it for a stool.

"Alright, let's get this slumber party started," Roland said as he sprung up to run to the carriage. "I'll be right back," he called over his shoulder.

Crouching down, I stroked a spark with my flint and iron, blowing on the dead brush and causing the flames to ignite. I placed more sticks until the flames grew large enough for one of the larger pieces of wood Roland found earlier. The other knights made their own campsite a few yards away. They stayed to themselves, but I was sure they were watching my every move to report to the King if needed. Roland walked back to the campfire with a lute in hand, and I huffed a laugh.

"See, you already know what's happening." He pointed a finger at me before plopping back down on his makeshift stool, setting his instrument on his knee. Roland used to play all the time during the calm days of the war. It helped everyone to think more about the moment we were in rather than the situation. Harper stood up.

"I didn't know you played." She gave Roland a warm smile.

"It's been a while but I'll do my best for you, love." His voice full of admiration for Harper made her blush. Roland played as if he had never stopped, lightly plucking the strings, creating a melody full of delicacy and richness. He picked up the pace, causing Harper to jump on her toes. She pulled Myla up with her.

"Come on, let's make those memories right now." Myla brightened at that, and my heart swelled seeing her happy. Harper looped her arm around Myla's and they danced, twisting and twirling, to the rhythm of Roland's song, laughing. Hearing Myla's laugh was even more beautiful than the music. It had been so long since I heard it. Her real genuine laugh. I smiled to myself, admiring her dancing around the fire, and every time Harper twisted her around, she peered at me with that bright smile. Heat budded in the center of my chest, hotter than the fire itself. I looked away, trying to distract myself right when Roland finished the song he was playing. He bent down.

"I have another surprise." He pulled a bottle of something out from behind the log he had been sitting on. "What kind of party would it be without drinks?" He laughed a burley laugh before taking a swig from the bottle and handing it to me. I shook my head and passed it on to Harper. My head had quit hurting halfway through the ride to camp. I'd rather not have a repeat of that. Harper took a long swig and covered her mouth afterward with an unpleasant scowl on her face.

"Next time, dear, bring wine. This stuff is atrocious." She let out a giggle before handing it over to Myla who took a sip, making a face and then handing it back to Roland. He set it down and started playing another song. This song was slower, the tone darker, and I closed my eyes, brow furrowed by the memories—flashbacks.

The music played as images of blood, blades, and screams flashed under my lids. My hands clenched open and closed. I opened my eyes long enough to see Harper pull Myla up again, and they danced, sang, and drank. All the while, my mind froze; my body tensed. I grabbed the small piece of iron and squeezed it, trying to steady myself. My knuckles went white against the grip of the iron I palmed. The images didn't stop, and I squeezed harder. Myla's voice pulled me back as her warm touch grazed my arm.

"Gavin." Her voice startled me from my thoughts. A soft gasp left me, and as I looked around, Roland and Harper were looking at me, just as concerned as Myla was. The music had long stopped. The only sound was the crackle from the fire. I pulled away from Myla as I stood.

"Sorry, excuse me," I said quickly, setting my sights on the wood line. "I'm going on watch." I cleared my throat and hurried away. As I came out of my internal war, I tried to calm my racing thoughts. My mind wandered back to the Princess I wished were mine.

Chapter Seventeen

MYLA

I couldn't sleep. I had been tossing and turning in my bedroll for what felt like forever after the little party we had was over. Gavin hastily making his way into the woods was all I could think about. Was he okay? I glanced over to the other bedrolls, but I didn't see anyone sleeping in them. Harper and Roland must have run off together, and Gavin said he was going to be walking the perimeter for the night.

Where was he? I got up from the ground. The fire was almost out from the night's chill, making it almost impossible to see anything more than a few feet in front of me without its light. I made my way over to the carriage, stopping myself when I heard sounds of pleasure coming from inside it. Looked like I found Roland and Harper. Sounded like they were enjoying themselves. I let out a small laugh as my face reddened before continuing my walk into the woods for Gavin.

I walked back over to the campsite and grabbed a small shawl from my bag before I went into the dark woods. The chilled air lightly whipped my hair around and the frosted ground crunched as I walked on the narrowed path, passing through the giant pines of the woods. I stopped to admire their beauty. I had never been this far away from home, but I had never felt more alive, at peace, and free.

The stars were bright in the sky, and I could feel the smile pull up on my lips. The only place I had ever walked was the gardens in Baela, and although the roses and wildflowers that grew there were beautiful, nothing compared to the beauty out here. I kept trekking the path lit by the moonlight while admiring all the pretty things surrounding me, down to the very smell. I heard a slight movement of the brush in the distance but dismissed it as a small animal of some sort when I was startled by a familiar voice.

"Trying to catch mice in the middle of the night again?" I turned around, seeing Gavin looking down at me atop his horse, bareback, with a sleepy smile. He looked as handsome as ever with his black tunic. It was slightly undone, revealing his chest, adding to his captivating looks. The only armor I saw was his thick leather gauntlets. I was sure his sword would be strapped to his side though. But past the smile, I could tell he was tired.

"Actually, yes, they are quite the listeners." He huffed a laugh at that and hopped down off the horse effortlessly.

"You really should be back at camp, Myla. It can be dangerous out here. At least at camp Roland can keep you safe. I have little trust in the others."

"Me either, but I'm not too sure about that." I gave him a side-eye.

"What do you mean?" He furrowed his brow at me.

"I caught him and Harp... you know." His eyes widened with his grin.

"Ah, well." We laughed at the thought of how they ended up together through us. "I'll make a note to send him on the perimeter watch next time—" He looked down at that last part as if wondering if there ever would be a next time.

"Are you alright? You seemed... out of it at camp."

"I'm fine." His response was quick, to the point. I turned to start walking again, but he caught my hand. "Myla... I... have flashbacks sometimes."

"Of the war?" I asked, and he nodded, but I didn't push any further. "Well, if you ever want to talk about it, I'm here." I gave his hand a light, reassuring squeeze before releasing it. Matching his stride, I walked next to him as he guided his horse along.

"Question for a question?" I asked, and he gave me that side smile I loved.

"Go for it," he said while tugging on the bridle of the horse to keep him moving.

"Do you ever see yourself having children?"

"Diving right in, huh?" He smiled at me again. "Uh, yeah, if I found the right person, I'd want to have a family someday." He peered over at me. "My turn, do you have any passions? Hobbies?"

"I only learned things to pass the time, like sewing, and occasionally I liked to read if I could get my hands on a good book. I always wanted to learn how to ride but I was told my whole life it's improper for a lady to ride a horse." I took a step toward the horse, stroking his nose.

"Do you want to learn?" He nodded toward the horse and then back to me.

"I—I don't even know how to get on him."

"It's okay. I'll help you." He guided me to the side of the horse, putting his hands on my hips, making my breath hitch in my chest at his touch. We had not been close since his encounter with my father, which he wouldn't talk about. Helping to lift me onto the horse was a little unsteady at first, but he calmed quickly.

"What's his name?"

"Maximus, but everyone calls him Max. " The excitement rolled over me as I patted Max's neck, and Gavin guided him forward. I was riding a horse. I stretched out my arms on either side, feeling the breeze as Gavin led us.

"Where are we going?" I asked through my smile.

"You'll see," he said, looking ahead to the wooded trail. We traveled for minutes filled with tensed silence before he finally spoke again.

"We're here." He turned to me, offering me his hand to get down. The woods were less dense where he had taken us, and I could see mountains in the distance lit by the full moon's glow with a steep fall just in front of us, leading to the valley below. The view was beautiful. Gavin released my hand after I slid off Max and walked over to the flat ground before the decline and sat there. I followed suit and did the same. Sitting next to him, we both watched the blanket of stars twinkle in the endless night sky.

"What are we doing?" I asked, keeping my eyes set on the view in front of me.

"Waiting," he said, not looking in my direction either. I finally glanced at him. He had been so distant lately and it brought a dull ache to my chest.

"For?" I questioned

"Your favorite colors." His comment brought a faint smile to my lips as I looked forward at the sight of the skies slowly changing from the darkness of night to the blues, pinks, and oranges of early morning. The sun's rays began cresting over the distant mountain tops, showering their light down upon the valley. I leaned into my knight, laying my head against his shoulder. I accepted the moment he was giving me—giving us—to be together. I intertwined my fingers with his as we sat there together in utter silence. I wouldn't let whatever my father had said or done interfere with this moment. That conversation was meant for another day.

Roland's hostile voice echoed through the trees behind us, causing Gavin to lurch up to his feet, grab my arm, and pull me up with him. He rushed us forward toward Max and leaped onto him, effortlessly offering me his forearm to join him. I followed suit with the motions he did. I wasn't nearly as graceful, but I made it atop Max before Gavin bolted him toward the sounds of Roland's voice. Within minutes, we were almost at camp, and I could hear the screams of men trying to give orders while others screeched out in pain. Blood tinged the air as swords rang against each other.

I heard a snarling laugh and heavy booted footsteps, and before I knew it, Maximus was rearing up, throwing me off of him.

"Myla!" I heard Gavin's voice, but it sounded distant before my hearing came back. The pain in my head pounded. I felt his hands hauling me back to my feet as I put together what happened.

We were being ambushed. Ferand's loyal ones, I presumed.

Gavin pushed me behind him as the man that spooked Max swung his sword. Gavin unsheathed his with precision, blocking the goon's blow. I looked around at the scattered bodies lying on the ground. Some knights still lay in their bedrolls with their throats sliced, never getting the chance to fight back, while only a few remained alive, fighting off whatever enemies were lurking in the forest. They were sneak attacking everyone, but as the sun's rays began shining through the trees, more and more men slowly came into view. I saw Roland a short distance away, fighting beside a few knights from camp, until one after the other slowly fell as arrows flew through the trees with a force to kill.

"Roland!" I yelled a warning to him as the arrows came closer and closer to where he was. But he wasn't able to escape all of them. A single arrow jutted out from his shoulder as he tried to evade them. One barely missed his neck as he darted behind a tree. A heavy breath escaped me as I tried to calm my racing heart.

I looked to my bedroll where my pack lay with my sword's hilt peeking through the top. Gavin fought fearlessly with the man in front of him. The man was rugged with dark skin, as if he had been traveling under the sun for days—maybe months. He carried a stench that conveyed he hadn't bathed for a time. None of the goons were wearing armor. They wore tattered, normal clothes with small packs while carrying swords and arrows on their backs. But they weren't unrehearsed in the ways of combat.

Gavin never let the man through as they battled. I waited for my opening and took it when it arose. Gavin screamed at me, but I didn't look back. My eyes focused on my sword, and my feet slammed against the moist soil.

I could feel the closeness of my enemy behind me as I leaped for my sword, yanking it free from my pack as I spun back and smacked against the ground, knocking the breath from my already burning lungs. I held up my sword with shaking arms right when the man hauled his over his head, readying himself to unleash death down upon me. But warm blood seeped through my clothes as it rained from the man's gut from where Gavin's sword jutted through him. Gavin released his sword, pushing the unnamed man to the side, and hauled me into his arms, palming his bloodied hands against my face, pushing his forehead against mine.

"Are you out of your mind?" His breath was jagged, filled with so much concern. After a few moments of nothing but the sounds of our breathing and the beating of my heart ringing in my ears, Gavin helped me stand on unsteady legs. I looked over our camp with the eerie silence of death looming over the ground. Knights lay scattered, some still twitching in their last moments of life.

At least twenty invaders lay dead beside them. Any that were left must have retreated into the woods once the sun was high in the sky. Roland stumbled through the tree line in front of us with Harper beside him. Part of the arrow was still sticking out of his shoulder. I rushed forward with bloodied, tear-trailed cheeks and wrapped Harper into my arms. She released a loud sob as if she had been holding it in until the battle was over. A beat later, I was examining Roland.

"I'm fine. Are you?" he questioned, looking down at the blood on the front of my clothes.

"Not mine."

"Good," he responded with a nod toward Gavin, as if letting him know he was okay too. They had been friends so long they could communicate with each other through looks alone. I hastily made my way toward the carriage, where we had a medkit. My hands were still shaky as I opened it, looking for threads and needles.

The arrow went clean through his shoulder. Finding what I needed, I returned to Roland who was now sitting on the same tree stump he used as a stool last night, leaning over with his elbows resting on his knees. Harper had helped him by slicing his shirt off with a small dagger she still had grasped in her hand. I looked at the arrowhead sticking out of his back and called Gavin over.

"I need you to pull it out." I talked to him in a hushed whisper.

"You know, I can hear you," Roland spoke, lifting his head over his shoulder with a huff and a side smile.

"Sorry," I said as Gavin grabbed a bottle of amber liquid from the ground and handed it to Roland.

"Take a few swigs," Gavin spoke, giving Roland's uninjured shoulder a light squeeze. "It's going to hurt, brother." Roland took a long swig from the bottle, causing bubbles to rise as the contents of the bottle slowly emptied until only a sliver was left behind. Roland caught his breath from the searing alcohol before he spoke again.

"Now," Roland said the same moment Gavin wrapped his calloused hand around the arrowhead and ripped it from his shoulder in one pull. Roland's yell was rugged before he cursed under his breath. I grabbed the bottle and poured the last bit of alcohol over his wounds. His grunts of pain came out labored as he tried to catch his breath. Harper gripped his hands as I shoved the needle through and began closing the gaping holes in his shoulder. His breathing slowed as more time passed while I started stitching the second opening. He kept his eyes closed—focused until I was finally done with his sutures.

Roland stood, and Harper wrapped her arms around him. Roland sagged into her embrace before they separated, and we all walked back to the carriage. Without missing a beat, Gavin began loading up camp. He hooked the horses up to the carriage and grabbed our packs and bedrolls.

Roland rested in the carriage with Harper. Once he was finished packing, Gavin started gathering the bodies of the fallen and placing them next to each other, dragging them one by one. I helped him move them. I didn't want him to face this alone. These men were his comrades. I was sure he had known their names and shared times of war together with them.

Gavin's expression was grave as we placed the last few men next to each other. I didn't need him to tell me he was hurting. I saw the raw emotions through every tick of his jaw and the blank, pained stare on his face as he looked over the men he once knew. How many had he lost along his life filled with duty and war? It seemed never-ending.

I wrapped my arms around him in his silent grief and he gently pulled me in, accepting my comfort before we walked back to the carriage and moved on through the rest of the day. The only knights that lived were Gavin and Roland.

Nightfall came quickly and quietly. Gavin said nothing as he sat ramrod straight on high alert while holding the reins and guiding the horses through the terrain and trees. As the sun's rays disappeared, Gavin brought the carriage to a stop between a small clearing that sat between the wall of mountains on either side of us. I didn't hesitate. I hopped down from the box seat next to him and opened the carriage door to check on Roland's wounds.

Roland had his head leaned back against his seat with his eyes closed while Harper's head lay in his lap while he ran his fingers tenderly through her wavy red hair. He turned his head toward me, peeking an eye open.

"How are you feeling?" I asked quietly as Harper slept.

"Like I got speared with an arrow." He gave me a grin and I rolled my eyes at his wisecrack.

"I'll live, Your Highness, all thanks to your handy work." He tilted his head with a wink, speaking again in a jesting manner as if I were a mothering hen that kept checking her eggs.

"Okay, sir knight. Have you ever considered being a jester? It would seem to fit you well," I said, and he let out a light chuckle, doing his best not to wake Harper.

"How is she?" I asked, following his gaze down to the woman lying in his lap.

"She was exhausted. She didn't get much..." He trailed off a moment before catching eyes with me again. "...sleep last night, and then today, she stayed up worried while I slept." He quirked his lips

"I'm sure you both didn't get much sleep last night," I said while giving him a knowing look. He let out another chuckle, not meeting my eyes at my half-hearted confession of catching them in the act.

Slowly, I shut the carriage door with a small click before turning around to see Gavin gathering wood from the grounds where we would camp. The chill had already set in for the night. It seemed to get colder the deeper we traveled through the mountain pass. I gathered a few smaller sticks, making my way toward him as he crouched on the ground, using some dead grasses to get the embers of a fire started with his flint and iron.

I grazed my hand along his forearm while he worked, and he flinched. His head jerked in my direction. His eyes were wide as he let out a steadying breath. It was as if he were waking from a nightmare while being awake. I wondered if he had been in the midst of flashbacks all day. The thought brought an ache to my chest for not reaching out to him sooner.

"Hey—" He cut me off.

"I'm fine."

"It's okay to not be." He looked over to me at that, and his eyes softened.

"I have to be."

"No, you don't, not always." He huffed a laugh under his breath at my response.

"How do you do it?" he asked as his face grew more serious.

"Do what?"

"Be fine after everything you endured in that castle."

"Because on the days I wasn't, I leaned on those who were." He just shook his head, looking back down at the embers that were now glowing amid the browning brush. A brief pause stretched between us before I spoke again.

"I'm here if you need me to be; if you want me to be." Silence lingered for another moment as Gavin added wood to the growing fire before he began speaking.

"My father and I got separated that day. Bodies littered the ground both from our side and from the other kingdoms. I fought my way through every sword, every man that came for me..." He trailed off in thought, looking into the flames as if he could picture the memory. Firelight danced along the planes of his face as he went on. "I remember when I found him amongst those already gone. He was close to death himself. There was so much blood. I couldn't tell the difference between his, mine, and others. The last thing he wanted to say I refused him because I wanted to believe I could save him, and when I couldn't... He saved me." He looked down at the soil, not allowing me access to his face. I palmed his cheek, pulling his tear-rimmed eyes back to mine. He had been holding this inside, reliving it alone, blaming himself for a death he couldn't prevent.

"Because your father loved you, he wouldn't want you holding on to this grief."

"It should have been me." A lone tear slipped down his face. His eyes never left mine.

"No, Gavin... Your father knew he was already gone. He saved you knowing that fact." His shoulders drooped at my words. I wrapped my arms around him, pulling him into the crook of my neck. I felt his body relax for the first time today.

His arms wrapped around my waist, going up my back. We clung to each other as the fire crackled and popped. This was the most he had touched me in the last few weeks of him maintaining the distance between us. When he released me, he placed his forehead against mine and palmed my face before leaning in and placing a soft kiss on my lips. I reveled in his every touch. Returning his movements, I deepened the kiss.

I wrapped my arms around his neck to pull him closer to me. Grabbing my hips, he pulled me onto his lap. His length hardened in his trousers against my inner thigh. The feel of him made a small moan escape me as our kisses became frenzied. Our tongues collided as he tangled his fingers into the hair at the nape of my neck.

Wood snapped from a few feet away, causing Gavin's mouth and hands to still. We both stopped and looked to the right of where we sat entwined with one another. Roland and Harper stood there both wearing smug grins on their faces at what they were seeing.

"Looks like you're not getting much sleep either," Roland said in a matter-of-fact tone as Gavin released me from his hold.

"We brought dinner from the carriage," Harper spoke, trying to sound optimistic.

"I'll get the bedrolls," Gavin said, looking away from me as he stood once again, putting up the barrier that I had felt was just falling away. He placed his walls up again, one stone at a time. My heart sank further into my gut when he returned and placed his bedroll on the opposite side of the fire from me.

Roland and Harper sat together, practically sharing a bed as they ate some bread and dried meats we brought for the trip. I turned away from the fire and the people that surrounded it.

Chapter Eighteen

MYLA

I awoke suddenly to a hand covering my mouth as I fought the urge to squeal.

"Shhh." Gavin tried to silence my worries, but his reassurance didn't last long as he pointed a single finger toward the tree line closest to us. Gleaming eyes met mine.

A wolf.

He was thin, probably starving as the smaller animals of the woods burrowed when winter approached. His snarl in our direction made me jump. I looked over to where Roland and

Harper had lay, but it seemed they had made their way back to the carriage in the middle of the night. Figured.

Gavin wrapped his arm around my waist and we slowly stood together. I wanted to push him away, and if we weren't in this situation, I would have. I was mad at the distance he had been keeping between us since the night of the ball. But between a rabid starving wolf and Gavin, I'd take the latter.

Gavin slowly backed us away from the animal. I wondered what he was doing until I noticed Max behind us. His ears were flat against his head, sensing the danger and uncertainty from the beast in front of us.

"When I say run, you run." His whisper slid over my neck as I nodded in understanding. He braced me against his chest as he took three more steps backward toward our bareback escape waiting for us.

"Wait," I whispered, staring at my pack that had been left on my bedroll. I had used it as a pillow against the cold ground.

"Leave it." Gavin's whisper was firm, but I didn't listen. I took one last look at the wolf as I pushed out of Gavin's hold, lunging for my pack. Ripping it from the bedroll, looping my arm through the strap, I turned to run to Max. Somehow Gavin had already leaped atop him in my haste of grabbing my things. His arm was outstretched as he yelled for me.

"Hurry!" I latched on to him, pulling myself onto Max. Gavin grabbed my hips, yanking me into his lap. He didn't hesitate, directing Max into a fast gallop through the dense trees off the path. Limbs from low-hanging branches lashed at us as we rushed forward. More wolves slowly emerged from either side of the tree line, nipping at our heels, glaring at us with snarled smiles and glowing eyes as we tried to escape.

I was too scared to look back at the roaring growls and barks of the wild animals growing louder behind us as Max rushed forward. I pushed my rear into Gavin's lap, gripping Max with my legs, tucking myself down toward his neck. I was shuddering from the adrenaline pumping through my veins. Max was running so fast the only sound was the whistle of wind blowing past my face. The chill in the air felt as though it were going straight through my body regardless of the thick shawl I was wearing. There had to have been at least twelve sets of eyes. The picture in my head made me shudder.

"What are we going to do!?" I yelled over my shoulder to him.

"There is a river up ahead. If we cross, we'll lose them!" he shouted back, pushing Max faster than I had ever seen any horse go.

"What about Harp and Roland!?" I questioned.

"They'll be fine. I trust Roland." At one moment, I could hear the rushing river flowing. The next Maximus was plunging us into the chilling waters.

Gavin and I got off of him so he could move easier through the strong current as we held onto his bridle, pulling him forward through the wide river. Halfway through, we heard the wolves snarling about their dinner escaping them.

Looking over my shoulder, I saw them pacing along the river's edge, looking at us with dark, beady eyes full of hunger. My feet kept sinking into the bottom of the river with every step as I pushed my legs forward. I threw myself down in the dirt with breaths so heavy my lungs ached. My skin pebbled as the brisk air rushed over me. Gavin leaned up, looking at the other side of the river before glancing over to me and getting to his feet.

"Come on, we have to get out of the cold." He grabbed my hand, helping me up before we got back on Max. I slouched in between Gavin's arms, the exhaustion settling into my bones as he guided Max through the woods back to a trail.

I leaned my head against him, the cold tingling sensation growing in my limbs with every step Max took. There was a small cave along the mountainside where Gavin stopped. My fingers and toes were numb by the time I got off of Max. My insides were cold. I couldn't tell if the shivers were from the chill or from my body craving something more than just warmth. Gavin gathered sticks and brush for a fire. His clothes clung to his chiseled body. I couldn't stop my eyes from roaming over him before going into the cave.

Gavin returned a few moments later and quickly started a fire while I sat ringing out my long hair and piling it back on top of my head. The warmth of the flames fought off the chill from my skin. He came to my side hastily, pulling my face into his stiff hands.

"Are you alright?" I could read the concern in his voice.

"Yes, I'm okay, just cold." My teeth chattered. He took his hands away and pulled his tunic over his head.

"Take your clothes off." My cheeks reddened and my eyes widened. "We need to use each other's body heat to stay warm." He unbuttoned his pants, pulling them down, and it took every fiber of my being to not glance down.

My eyes roamed over his body everywhere but there before I fiddled with the straps on my bag, setting it next to the fire to dry. His eyes met mine in the dim firelight, and it was like I could see all of my burning desires within them.

I pulled my heavy, wet shawl and dress off my shoulders and down to the floor, with nothing left to cover me, and placed them next to my bag. I was laid completely bare to Gavin once more. We lay down next to the fire with him nestled behind me, and he wrapped his arms around me. I wasn't cold for much longer.

The heat pooled in my center with his hands wrapped around my body. I tried to keep myself from trembling under his touch. Maybe I could lie and tell him it was from the cold, but I doubted he would believe me. My body tingled everywhere our skin was touching. The excitement was unbearable as I thought about his hands on me, pleasuring me. My heart was pounding so loud in my ears that I felt like the entire Kingdom of Baela could hear it. Gavin pulled me back. His front was completely flush against my back, and I had to distract myself before I lost all control.

"Question for a question," I said, voice trembling. I was so lost in the sensation of his body pressed against mine, I barely recognized my voice. He whispered in my ear.

"I believe it was my turn." I nodded my head in anticipation of his question. "If you were truly free to make your own decisions, what would you choose?"

I lay there a moment, building up the courage to tell him about the deepest, darkest parts of my feelings for him, but all I could do was turn over to meet his mirrored gaze. His lips were so close his warm breath caressed my cheek. I couldn't control my desires any longer. I cupped his face and pulled his mouth to mine, and his arms tightened around me as my core flooded. I ran one hand down his muscled chest, past his trousers to palm his hardened length. He let out a groan of pleasure between our passionate, wet kisses. He grabbed for my wrists, taking both of my hands, placing them both above my head, and pinning them there with one strong motion.

"Myla, I want you more than my body needs breath. I've never wanted anything more than you—" He paused for a moment. "—but we can't." He closed his eyes as if trying to fight his own desires.

"Then let's make the best of what we can do," I rasped next to his ear, trailing kisses down his neck. I tugged my hands free, bringing the same hand that he used to hold me captive down my body, slipping his hand between my legs. "Even if I can't have all of you." I left his hand there, meeting his eyes full of restraint, but as he leaned over resting on his elbow, palming my center, sensing how ready I was for him, he gave in. I let out a moan from his touch, and the sensation climbed within me.

I took my hands and pulled out his hard length, stroking him. He went rigid against my touch. His groan of need almost made me come undone. He slid his fingers over the small bundle of nerves between my thighs, making me clench my legs together as he stroked me. I moaned for him as he swallowed the sounds between our fiery kisses.

My body melted into his touch. I arched my back against his hand, wanting more, pleading for it while I stroked him faster. He plunged his fingers into me and I cried out, throwing my head back into the building bliss within me.

Gavin kissed my neck, down to my breast, suckling and circling his tongue around my peaked nipple. I wrapped both hands around his shaft, stroking him as he moved his fingers deeper—faster while using his thumb to circle my sensitive bulb of nerves. I grounded myself harder against him, wanting more.

I needed it. I needed him.

He pumped his fingers faster, and I couldn't control my movements anymore as I arched against him. We both pushed and pulled against that raging edge. Our breaths quickened.

"Myla." Hearing my name on his lips filled with his guttural arousal pushed me over the edge. I couldn't stop the wave of ecstasy that washed over me. He took in my cry of pleasure with another kiss, and I felt his warm release slide over my hands.

Gavin palmed me until my moans turned into heavy breaths. He took his hand out from between my thighs. I grabbed my dirty dress on the ground next to me to clean up before curling back up next to the fire with Gavin lulling me to sleep against his broad chest.

Chapter Nineteen

Gavin

I looked down at the face of the woman I loved, beaten and bloodied, lying on my lap and gasping for breath as blood trickled from the corner of her mouth. My eyes lined with tears as I rocked my body back and forth, trying to calm my frantic nerves while telling her everything was going to be okay when I knew it wasn't.

He did it. He killed her, and all I could do was hold her as she left this world. My chest was heavy, and I felt the crushing pain of a boot against it, knocking me back as Fredrick yanked Myla from my arms, throwing her to the side like trash. I looked up into the eyes of the man responsible. King Henry stared down at me with deadened eyes. No emotion, no feeling, no guilt for anything he had ever done to anyone.

"Gavin, what happened to a knight's chivalry?" He brought his heavy boot up again to my throat, and it was as if all the hours of training the muscles in my body did nothing for me as he pushed me into the cold ground. "Being with another man's promised?" He shook his head with distaste while Fredrick ticked his tongue at Henry's statement. "Now, you're going to get your punishment." Henry removed his boot from my neck and I gasped for breath, coughing from the lack of air in my lungs. He brought himself behind me, grabbing me by the hair and pulling my head up so my eyes aimed at Myla's mangled body in front of me a few feet away.

"I'm sorry, Myla." She opened her eyes filled with fear and I broke at the sight of her. Tears streamed down my face as I begged for her forgiveness. "I'm sorry I couldn't keep you safe, I—"

"Shhh," was all she could get out as I tried to fight against the hold of the ropes Frederick wrapped around my wrists. I pulled against Henry's grip on my scalp so hard my head felt like it was on fire. Fredrick grabbed her by the hair, pulling her limp body up so she was on her knees. I could hear her faint cries and I screamed.

"Stop! Please! I'll do anything."

"It's too late for that." Fredrick spoke with a smile, pulling a dagger from his belt and slashing Myla's neck. Her blood splattered across my face as her body thudded on the floor in front of me. The silence of death hit me. My ears rang, and my vision kept getting narrower and narrower on Myla's body growing cold in a pool of her own blood.

Henry let me go. No longer bound, I crawled to her. As I held her in my arms, I shattered. My screams reached the tops of the mountains of Baela.

Suddenly, it was gone: Myla, the blood, the horror, and I was faced with a new nightmare.

My family, my mother, stood there with all my siblings, flailing to fight off knights ordered to kill.

My body trembled as everyone I had ever loved slowly got picked off by royal knights, all the way down to my little sister. I sat there, wrists bound, looking at everyone I loved dead in front of me, covered in their blood. I fell to the ground, feeling my heart crumble into a million pieces.

"Gavin!" Myla's voice pulled me out of the nightmare. My hands clenched tight around her wrists, too tight. It left a mark when I released her.

"Myla, I'm sorry—" She brought her hands up to cup my face.

"Are you alright?"

"Y-yeah." I fumbled over my words, but I told her a half-truth. "I was having nightmares from the war." I grabbed her hands, gently placing them back down to her sides before getting up. I grabbed my dry clothes, noticing that the sun was already high in the evening sky. We slept straight through the day from exhaustion. I kept my eyes turned away from Myla. "We should go. Get dressed, we're behind." Myla noticed my stern change.

"What's wrong?" she asked, but I stayed turned away, giving her some type of privacy regardless of our heated encounter from last night. I heard the shuffle of her bag as she spoke while getting dressed. "You can look at me, you know." But I didn't turn.

"Myla, we can't do this." I finally faced her.

"Gavin..." Her eyes brimmed with tears as she gripped my arm. I pulled away.

"We will continue this journey the way we started it. I am your knight for protection, and you are the future Princess of Credia. I will escort you to your new kingdom and then we will part ways."

"Why are you doing this?" Her voice cracked, and it gutted me.

"Because it's what's right. End of discussion." I spoke firmly, holding myself together even though I was in ruins on the inside.

Seeing her in the leathers I bought for her with her sword on her side, my heart clenched at how beautiful she looked in the evening's light. Her eyes showed me the hurt I was causing. It was for her own good, but it still made me question everything I was saying.

"You sound like my father." Her voice almost broke again, but she held herself together with her chin high.

"Myla—" I paused, looking down, asking myself if this was the right thing to do even though it felt so wrong. I knew it was what would keep everyone safe. "I don't want to jeopardize your life or anyone else's over my desperate heart. I hope one day you'll understand that."

She turned away, gathering up her bag as we walked out toward Maximus grazing near the tree I tied him to. I hauled myself on top of him, but Myla just looked ahead to the trail.

"Maybe I should walk."

"Myla, please stop this. Get on the damn horse," I said, extending my hand to her and trying to stay calm at the fact that she compared me to her horrible father. She stood there in contemplation for a moment before taking my hand and getting on Max as I led him into a trot down the eastern trail. My nerves grew with every step closer to town. The same town of my upbringing.

I did my best to focus on anything in front of me as Myla's hips rubbed against my thighs with every step Max took. After last night, it made it all the more difficult to keep my arousal in check. I tried to stay relaxed with my arms wrapped around Myla's middle, holding the reins, but my heartbeat matched the quick thrum of Max's hooves against the ground. The tension in the air between Myla and me was so thick I could make butter. With every slight movement, it was as if she nestled her rear harder between my thighs while she relaxed her back against my chest.

Was she doing this on purpose? Was this her retaliation for what I said? If so, it was working. This was agonizing.

I understood why she was mad. I was angry too. Did she really think I wanted to watch her marry another man and move on with her life without me in it? Neither of us had admitted to loving the other, and I wasn't sure when it happened for myself, when my heart desired more than just being her knight. I guessed it was more of an accumulation of things from the moment I met her on the outside of those gates.

Pulling myself from my thoughts, I saw the rooftops of houses in the distance along with the bustling townspeople up ahead, walking back and forth between the modest market at the entrance of my small town. I turned Max sharply to the left to avoid the crowd.

"Where are you going?"

"The back way, I'd just like to avoid any crowds for now." She was silent for a moment and then went rigid while turning her head toward me.

"This is your hometown, isn't it?!" She smiled proudly, showing me her excitement. How this woman instantly made all the nerves fall away for a moment amazed me. She held my hands, and I realized I had been gripping the reins so tightly my hands ached as they loosened at her touch. Suddenly, all the tension between us fell away the moment she realized where we were. Where I was.

"I'm here for you, if you want me to be." She repeated her sentiment from before at the same moment I saw the steeply gabled roof of my family's farmhouse. The home had never been big. My brothers and I always shared a room until we got a little older and helped our father add on before the war started.

Looking at it from the short distance brought back so many memories. The lump in my throat made it impossible to breathe. I huffed a breath and closed my eyes, trying to hold myself together, writhing the reins between my fingers when I heard a familiar male voice yell across the way.

"Ma! Someone's here." It was a little deeper than I remembered—my younger brother. I slid off of Max, offering Myla a hand down as I walked across the large front yard of my home.

"Who is it, Wes?" My mother's voice called out as she walked out the front door wiping her hands on her flour covered apron. Her eyes widened as they met mine.

"Gavin..." She mouthed my name in disbelief as her eyes lined with tears.

"Hey, Ma." She ran down the steps toward me and threw her arms around me. A loud sob escaped her. I couldn't hold back the tears anymore. Her knees went weak, making us both fall to the ground. I sat in the tall grass with her. She pulled back, cupping my face in her hands, her face wet with tears.

"I thought I'd never see you again," she spoke barely above a whisper.

"I'm sorry, Mom, I tried to—"

"Shhh." She pulled me back into her grasp. "It's okay. I know what happened."

"How?" I pulled back, furrowing my brow at her.

"Roland... he told us everything. Don't be mad at him, but he's kept in touch with us this whole time, letting us know how you were doing after the war, after your father—" Her chin trembled as she grabbed at her chest, her body crumpling in on itself. She took a few deep breaths, trying to steady herself. "Gavin, I want you to know that, no matter if it's been seven years or seven moments, I love you the same as I did the day I brought you into this world, and I would've made the same choice your father did."

The emptiness of my father's death filled me as the weight of surviving the tragedy lifted off my shoulders from my mother's reassurance. "I don't blame you, darling. I'm devastated because you had to endure it alone." I took in a deep, pained breath, feeling the tightness in my chest ease as the regret of not coming home sooner sunk into the knots in my stomach. My shoulders sagged as my mother lifted my chin.

"Hey, you're here now; that's all that matters." My eyes wandered to the three figures still standing on the porch, all with teary-eyed smiles on their faces, waiting their turn. Mom turned toward them, nodding for them to come over, and they all took off in a sprint. I quickly stood and prepared myself for their forceful embraces.

The love of my family surrounded me. Looking over my brothers' shoulders, I saw Myla standing there with her silent support, smiling at me and mouthing, "I told you so." Her eyes brimmed with tears. I couldn't remember the last time I allowed myself to feel anything about my father's death, but I had finally found some peace.

Chapter Twenty

MYLA

Before his mother noticed my presence, Gavin held out his hand, introducing me.

"Mother, this is Myla, the Princess of Baela, future to Credia." And her eyes widened with panic as her hands straightened her dirtied dress.

"Gods, Gavin, you brought royalty here. Your Highness—I—" She bowed quickly. "Please excuse the mess." She continued while looking at her feet. I placed my hand on her shoulder.

"Please, it's alright. Myla is fine. It's lovely to meet you." I spoke with a warm smile, trying to ease her nerves.

"I'm Beth. These are my children, Wesley, Beckett, and Jocelyn. It seems you're already acquainted with my eldest."

"Yes, you raised a fine gentleman." She glanced over at him with a side-eye that said he better be. My lips pulled up into a smile.

"Come now, dinner is almost ready. We'd love to have you." She grabbed Gavin's hand. "Both of you," she spoke kindly.

"Thank you," I said, and we all walked towards the front door as the smell of roasted chicken escaped the small cottage home. The smoke from the chimney barreled into the sky. We stepped through the open door, and the floorboards creaked under my feet. The kitchen and living area were open and quaint. They had already set the small round kitchen table for four with a whole chicken placed in the center surrounded by mixed vegetable sides and bread rolls. Beth made haste to the kitchen to grab more plates and silverware, while Wesley, Beckett, and Jocelyn sat down in their normal seats.

"So are you really a princess?!" Jocelyn asked with excitement filling her tone.

"Jocelyn, let's leave Her Highness alone, shall we?" Beth spoke up while placing our plates on the table.

"No, really, it's fine," I said to Beth, recognizing the whole family was nervous about a royal being in their presence. "Yes, I am a real princess." Her eyes lit up with joy.

"I've always wanted to meet a real princess! I'd love to be one someday!" "And who says you aren't?" I questioned with a smile.

"I'm just a poor farm girl. I could never be a princess," she responded, looking down at her plate while her mother filled it with chicken and veggies. Her mouth tugged into a frown at the thought of not having riches.

"You, my dear, can be anything you dream to be. Royalty and riches mean nothing. It's what's in here that matters," I said, pointing to my heart. Beth took her seat, glancing over at me with wonder in her eyes while Beckett and Wesley looked at each other. I took note of everyone's surprise as Gavin glanced over his family and then smiled to himself while looking back down at his plate, now overfilled with food. "What?" I said to no one in particular. "Is something wrong?"

"No, darling,.We're just all taken back, is all," Beth spoke for everyone.

"By what?"

"Why, you, dear... Have you ever met a person of royalty in this day and age? You act nothing like them. It's certainly odd for someone of such high regard to be—"

"What?" I said while shoveling some chicken into my mouth. It was perfectly seasoned and moist on my pallet. It was delicious and the first thing I'd eaten in over a day. I had to hold back a hum from how amazing it was. "By the way, the dinner is lovely, Mrs. Dawson. Thank you," I said in between bites. Her mouth parted in awe before she gave me a smile.

"They weren't expecting you to be kind." Gavin stepped in while tearing his buttered roll in half and eating it.

"In layman's terms, yeah," Beth said while picking at the chicken on her plate. Beckett waved his fork in our direction with a mouth full.

"So, does this mean you're going to stay for the potluck festival tomorrow, Gavin?" he asked.

"Manners," Beth said while giving Beckett a side glance filled with enough parental venom it could kill a man.

"Unfortunately, we should really—"

"Of course, we'll stay for the potluck." I cut off Gavin's statement, and he looked at me with his jaw clenched.

"Myla, we really should get back on the road. We are already behind schedule," Gavin said while Wesley cleared his throat. I was sure he, along with everyone else, sensed the tension building in the room.

"Yes, but as the Royal Princess of Baela, I want to stay for this potluck." My voice was stern as my eyes found Gavin's.

"Really, Myla—Your Highness, it's fine. It's just a gathering we have every year. It's nothing special. I'm sure you have more important things to tend to." Beth stumbled over her words nervously.

"Well, I don't get out much, Mrs. Dawson, and I really want to make the most of this trip, so we're staying." I would not let this go. I had put more emphasis in my tone when I said "making the most of this trip." Wesley got up, taking his plate to the sink.

"I'm going to go do the last of my chores, Ma. I'll be back. Good to see you home, Gavin," he said while walking toward the front door. He gripped Gavin on the shoulder as he passed by. "Pleasure to meet you, Myla." He left with that, letting go of Gavin and walking out the screen door.

"Pleasures all mine." I spoke up right before the screen slapped shut. Staring back at Gavin, I saw he was trying to hide the fury in his eyes, and failing at it.

"Momma! I get to go to the festival with Gavin and a real princess!?" Jocelyn was so excited there was no way I was going to miss out on this now. After we all finished up, Beth rose and gathered up the plates, and I stood to help her. I brought all the dishes to the sink already filled with cold water, but I didn't see a faucet anywhere.

"How do you get water?" I asked, and Beth, Jocelyn, and Beckett looked at me, surprised, before looking away.

"We have to fetch it from the well, dear. We don't have running water, but I'm sure I can do my best to accommodate you still." Beth spoke up next to me.

"Beth, you welcoming me into your home is more than enough accommodation." She smiled at that, and Gavin got up from his seat.

"It's been a long day, Ma. Where should we sleep tonight?"

"Well, the house has four rooms. Wesley and Beckett share one, while Jocelyn is in another. We haven't touched your room since the day they sent you away. You both are more than welcome to it." She regarded the tension between Gavin and me from her statement as her eyes bounced between us. "Or the living room or the loft in the barn. There's a cot up there." Beckett got up.

"I'm going to go help Wes bring in the cattle." Beckett gave his mother a quick kiss on the cheek before scurrying toward the door. "See you later Gavin, good to have you home," he said over his shoulder with a smile. Gavin nodded to him before turning back to his mother.

"Myla can take my room. I'll stay out here." He gestured toward the living room.

"Actually, could I stay in the loft? I'm sure Maximus would love the company," I said while eyeing Gavin, my features cold.

"Mother, could you excuse us?"

"Of course," Beth said nervously with a small bow of her head, grabbing Jocelyn by the hand before stepping outside.

"What is your problem!?" he yelled in a hushed tone.

"What problem?" I asked calmly.

"Staying for the potluck tomorrow? Keeping Max company? Don't play coy, Myla. You know we are behind."

"Well, I'd rather sleep with the horses tonight than spend another moment in here with you. I don't care how behind we are; I told you I wanted to make the most of this trip and I meant it." I spewed my words, turning away from him and stomping out of the front door, slamming the screen behind me.

Jocelyn and Beth were sitting on the porch swing together, and I gave them a forced smile, looking out toward the barn in the distance and starting toward it without missing a beat. I heard

Gavin's footsteps following and without turning, I spoke over my shoulder. "Leave me be, Gavin." His steps faltered.

I walked into the barn, meeting a few unfamiliar faces until I found Max eating in his stall. He looked up at me with a loud neigh before going back to his hay, and it made me smile even in the sad situation I was in. I ran my hand across his strong neck until I spotted the ladder, and I climbed up to the loft where there was a small wood furnace filled with leftover ash and a cot lying low on the floor with a light blanket across it, and I kicked myself for not asking for a warmer blanket.

There was no way I'd be going back in there after the spat between Gavin and me. The pit in my stomach grew and the knot in my throat swelled as I lay down on the bed surrounded by the evening's chill sweeping through the slats of the old barn. I wrapped the thin blanket around myself and let the emptiness consume me. Hot tears streamed down my face as I sobbed into my hands. I didn't know what to do anymore; I didn't want to marry Wyatt, I didn't want to go to Credia, and I didn't want to return to Baela.

I wanted to go wherever Gavin went. Society's standards could screw off, along with the duties I had to a kingdom that left me in the shadows my entire life. The only thing that I knew for certain was that I cared about Gavin, more than I was willing to admit aloud. But it seemed there was nothing I could do except watch my future, my freedoms, and a love I had dreamed of having go up in smoke.

I woke in the middle of the night to the warm glow of the wood furnace, wrapped in a heavy wool blanket that I didn't have when I went to sleep. I sat up, looking around the room with puffy eyes, confused, until I saw him. Gavin slept facing the opposite wall in a bedroll laid out on the hard wooden floor across from me in the loft. He didn't sleep in the living room. He must have snuck in here while I was sleeping. My heart clenched at this man's stubbornness, but also at the fact that he came in here and chose to be in the same room as me. To keep me warm in the midst of our fighting. The tears returned as I lay back down, wrapping myself in the thick covers. The burn started behind my eyes again.

"What's wrong?" His voice was a soft grumble over the crackle of the fire.

"You," I said.

"Me? What did I do now?" He questioned while turning over, lifting himself up on one of his elbows to look over at me with a teasing grin. I rolled my tear-lined eyes and huffed a sigh. He noted the tears in my eyes and his smile faded. "Myla, talk to me." His voice was soft.

"I can't." My voice broke over my words. He got up, crouching from the low roof in the loft, and walked over to me, sitting on the edge of my bed.

"Why can't you?"

"Because you are one of the only people I want to talk to, but also the one person I'm supposed to stay away from, and I don't know what to do about that."

"Pretend I'm someone else." He looked toward the fire burning in the furnace, and the soft glow of light showed me his handsome face. "Close your eyes and pretend I'm Harper. Tell me what you're feeling." I let out a small laugh at the image, but I did it anyway. I closed my eyes and started talking.

"This trip has made me feel in control of my choices. Over these past few days, I've been able to be who I want to be and not what society expects from me. I don't want to let that go, not yet, not ever."

"And what does that have to do with Gavin?" he murmured, and I opened my eyes. He was still staring at the fire until he saw me sit up. He peered over his shoulder at me.

"I don't want this to go away." He furrowed his brow while his lips parted.

"Don't want what to go away?" he questioned.

"This feeling—you're the only thing that's ever felt like mine."

"Myla." He closed his eyes and turned away from me, releasing a shaky breath.

"Gavin please—I—"

"Don't." He stopped me. "I won't let you spend the rest of your life hiding in the dark because of me."

"I don't mind the darkness, Gavin. I've learned that it can be beautiful when you have someone to share it with." I blew out the breath I was holding and turned away from him. Rolling over with nothing left to say, my last words rang true. I would spend the rest of my life with this man regardless of where we had to hide. Moments of tensed silence passed before his muscular arms encompassed me, pulling me into his warm embrace. His breath on my neck was calm and constant—home. He was the one I'd always choose.

Chapter Twenty-One

MYLA

The bed was already cold next to me where Gavin had slept. The fire was just hot embers left in the furnace, but it wasn't nearly as cold as it was during the night with the sun being out. Gavin never said another word last night after he crawled into bed with me, and it made me wonder if he felt the same. Was I his home too?

I got out of bed still wearing my leathers from the ride here and all I could think about was how much I wanted a bath. Stepping down the ladder into the barn, I noticed all the horses were gone.

My eyes adjusted to the morning light as I walked out into the open, finally getting to take in the beauty of this place.

Horses grazed the tall grasses in the open fields as the sky stretched so far that it met the land. The smell of salt and a scent I quickly recognized surrounded me, something warm and rustic. What I thought was the sky all along was the ocean in the distance, edged with woods. Its warm fragrance fell across the plains, and I realized it was as if the scent of Gavin's home clung to him all the way to my castle.

The thought of him made my lips tug up at the sides, and all I wanted to do was run down to the oceanside with him and bury my feet into the sand. I always dreamed of seeing the ocean, and it was so close now I could taste it in the air. I glanced towards the house, not seeing any activity from outside. I hadn't seen Gavin or his siblings anywhere. I walked up the stairs and lightly knocked on the door before hearing Beth's frantic voice from the other side.

"Come in! It's open!" I stepped in, hearing her hurried footsteps through the kitchen with the clanking sounds of pots and pans.

"Beth, do you need some help?" I asked as she hauled a giant bag of flour over her shoulder.

"Oh, don't you worry, dear. I think I got it," she retorted as she stumbled, dropping the bag of flour, and pots and pans crashed and clanked against the floor. I hurried over, picking them up.

"Here, I don't mind helping. What can I do?" I asked.

"Have you ever baked before?" I nervously bit my lip.

"No, but! I'm sure we could figure it out together." She gave me an optimistic smile.

"That sounds lovely. Your Hi—" She looked down to her feet before looking back to me. "Myla, that sounds lovely, Myla." I returned a smile at her correction. She was finally seeing me as a person rather than some stuck up royal. She rolled out what I assumed was going to be the base of the pie and added a sprinkle of the flour, and I followed the same steps she took. "You're a natural. I appreciate your help."

"It's no problem at all. So what are these for?"

"Every year for the potluck festival, everyone brings their own dish to add to the food stands. And this year I chose deserts like an idiot." I cackled at her tone.

"I guess deserts aren't your cup of tea?"

"No, absolutely not, I should have come up with something else. I've already burnt the last one." We both let out a laugh as we scooped the apple filling she had already put together into our own hollowed out pie crusts "Myla." I could tell from her change in tone that what she was going to say next wasn't going to be something I wanted to hear.

"I need to ask something of you."

"Okay... what's wrong?"

"I see the way my son looks at you. He's always been a boy that treads on thin ice. I know he's only been home for a day, but a mother knows these things..." She continued, "So I need you to promise me something." I looked to her in anticipation. "Promise me you'll leave him be. I mean no disrespect, but he's had enough loss in his lifetime and doesn't need to have his hopes held high for a princess already promised to another man."

"I mean no disrespect, Beth, but your son isn't a boy anymore. He's a grown man, and I believe he's plenty capable of choosing when he's had enough of something of his own accord." She gave me a small shake of her head while rolling out more dough for the next pies before looking back at me again.

"You're in love with him too, aren't you?" I met her eyes. Everything she already knew lay within that single glance. I finished laying the rounded flat top on the pie, adding the small vent holes to the top just like she did. When I turned to her, she pulled me into a warm hug.

"I'm so sorry, dear. I wish things were different for you, for you both. I couldn't imagine..." She trailed off as she released me, but all I could manage was a small smile, and I knew she understood.

"Thank you for your help," she said, peering up at me. "I can see why my son loves you."

"Oh, I don't know about that," I murmured, tucking my loose hair behind my ear.

"I do," she said, giving me a small smile and a wink. I could see where Gavin got some of his charm. Smiling, I looked down at how dirty I was before I changed the subject.

"Could you point me in the right direction for a bath?"

"Of course, the well is out back. I'm sure one of the boys out there can help you haul the water to the bathroom. If you need some new clothes to wear, I can find something for the potluck festival tonight."

"That sounds wonderful," I said, walking toward the back door. It creaked loudly as I stepped out. Wesley and Beckett, riding what I assumed were their own horses, raced through the open fields. I realized now why Gavin had offered me lessons. He grew up here on this beautiful oceanside farm. He could probably ride a horse before he could walk. Their home was smaller, but the love in the home made it all worthwhile. The snapping sound of cracked wood to my left pulled me from the far out views of the land. Gavin was chopping wood. The sweat from his labor made his white tunic with an opened front cling to his muscled body. He rolled up his sleeves before he continued.

Seeing him dressed casually and working hard turned my insides to mush without him saying a single word to me. I tried to remember how to breathe as my mind wandered back to the memories of that night, when his calloused hands caressed every part of me. The thought made my whole body tingle for his touch again. He wiped his brow and paused when he looked up, seeing me standing there admiring him.

"What are you up to, Princess?" he said with a lowered voice filled with a type of sultriness that made me tremble.

The blush coated my entire body at the way he looked at me, adding that wry smile as if he could see me trembling in the short distance. As if he knew what I had been thinking about.

"I wanted to ask if you'd help me haul water from the well?" I straightened my posture, trying to calm my racing heart.

"Of course." He slammed the ax into the wood, leaving it jutted up in the old stumped tree. We walked toward the well, and metal buckets were stacked next to it. He lowered them in one by one and then set them on the ground. "Let's see if all those training sessions paid off," he said, handing me two of the buckets to take to the bathing chambers. They pulled me down some at first but I grounded myself and hauled them up back to the house. Gavin walked with the buckets effortlessly, of course, like he had done it his whole life. Which now that I thought about it, he had. The water in my buckets sloshed around, while his had barely moved by the time we got to the tub.

"We'll make a few more trips and boil the other half so the bath is warm."

"Alright, while the water's boiling, are there any other chores that need to be tended to? I could help you." He shook his head with that crooked smile plastered on his face. "What's funny?" I asked as my lips turned up into a smile.

"Nothing... just pleasantly unexpected by you, again."

"I'm full of surprises." I looked at my feet. "Besides, it's the least I can do with how welcoming everyone has been." I peered back up at him, meeting his glossy gaze. His jaw ticked, almost as if what I said irritated him.

"Do you know how hard it is to resist you?" His voice was laced with frustration.

"Yes, because you're not the only one having to resist." He huffed a laugh at my response.

"What do you expect from me, Myla?!" He snapped, his tone was more passionate than indignant.

"I expect you to keep your word!" I exclaimed.

"And what word was that?"

"The night at the fountain, you told me we were going to make the best of the time we have left together, remember? What happened to that?! After the ball, you have been acting so distant, and then at the cave, I felt like I finally broke down your wall of resistance, just for you to shoot me down again! What happened to us, Gavin!?"

"I can't—" I cut him off

"Can't or won't? Tell me, what is it!?" I rushed him, my face merely inches from his. "Tell me, Gavin... what changed? Is it me?" I palmed his chest, and my eyes stung from the tears building behind them.

"No, Myla, it isn't you." He murmured, peering away from me a moment before finding my eyes again. "Your father told me to stay away from you and to get you to Credia, and if I didn't, he'd destroy everything I loved." He glanced around at his home and the precious people who dwelled there.

I let out a shuddering breath. "I'm sorry. Oh god, we should go—"

"Myla, stop, the potluck starts soon. We'll make the best of our time like I originally promised, and then we'll leave tonight.

Credia is just a day away." He tried to give me a reassuring smile, but I could tell he was tense about staying the rest of the day.

"Alright," I said, picking up my buckets and striding back to the well.

Sitting in the bath, the feeling of accomplishment washed over me. I spent the day with Gavin doing chores, and although my muscles were tired, I felt rewarded for doing everything on my own. Well, almost on my own. I soaked up every minute in the tub until the water grew cold before getting out.

I dried myself off, putting on the dress Beth had laid out for me. It was a long-sleeved, off-white dress with faded blue flowers detailed throughout the skirt. The fit was snug with a fabric corset, making the flow of the dress fit and flare out at my waist. It draped a little past my knees, but it probably would go down to Beth's ankles, considering how she was shorter than me.

I walked out of the bathing room, down the short, narrow hall, and into the living area where Beckett and Wesley were in the middle of a discussion. I stared at them a moment, realizing all the similarities between all three brothers. Wesley looked younger than Beckett, but not by much. He had the same light-brown hair as Gavin. He was shorter than Gavin and Beckett, more around my height, smaller too, more lanky, more boy-looking than man.

Wesley seemed more playful and less serious, unlike Beckett, who seemed to always be keeping himself busy with responsibilities around the farm. He had been so busy that this was the first time I'd seen him and got a better look at him while he wasn't working on something. His hair was darker, matching his dark brown eyes. His face was more rounded compared to Gavin's stronger jawline, and his complexion was slightly darker than all his other siblings, probably from always working outdoors.

I noticed Beckett and Jocelyn looked more like each other than Gavin and Wesley did, and I realized that Beckett and Jocelyn must look more like their father. Both had darker brown hair and brown eyes, unlike Gavin and Wesley, who took more back from Beth with her long dirty-blonde hair and blue eyes.

Beth kept her hair up in a messy braided crown on her head, but I could tell it would be long if she let it down. I was sure Beckett being the eldest son at home after Gavin and their father left for the war put a lot of pressure on him to take care of the family still at home. I felt bad for them. All of them had to grow up long before they should've had to. Over a selfish king's war for land and dominance. If I didn't already have reasons to hate my father enough, add that to the long list of things. Jocelyn came down the stairs, practically skipping with excitement, right when Gavin and his mother walked through the front door in deep conversation about something that seemed important.

"Come on, boys. Grab the pies and put them in the wagon. We must get going," Beth called to her younger sons, and they both obliged, quickly making way to the kitchen for the food she had prepared for tonight. They both glanced between Gavin and me when they walked by with grins on their faces.

Was it that obvious? This desire? This tension between Gavin and I as soon as our eyes caught each other. He cast his furtive glances at me. My heartbeat stumbled over itself again as a slow smile built on my face. Gavin wasn't wearing his armor, just a fitted long-sleeved white tunic with brown trousers. He dressed casually again, which made this feel more real. Were we going to pretend that this was real, just for tonight? Two normal people going to a festival and to hell with the responsibilities of everything else? I sauntered up to him as he held out his arm to escort me to the wagon.

"Myla," he murmured my name, almost to himself.

"Sir Gavin," I responded with a nod of my head and a small curtsy. He looked at me with his eyes filled with something I hadn't seen in what felt like forever—hope.

"Just Gavin is fine, for tonight." He gave me a wink and the finches flew in my stomach at that as I looped my arm with his and we headed off to the festival. Not as a princess and a knight, but as two people yearning to make the best of the time they had left together.

Chapter Twenty-Two

MYLA

The ride to the festival didn't take long. The wide road through town was just that: one road with small businesses on either side. While looking out toward the open land, my view was taken over by the cattle shoot of a town. Even with the setting sun, you could see the small cottage houses all on their own piece of land with their own livestock. There couldn't be much more than a hundred residents living out here.

Max trotted us through the town effortlessly, and I overheard Jocelyn in the back, rambling to her mother about all the fun games and sweets she was going to get to try. Passing down the wide road, I saw the last of the townspeople closing their businesses and turning their signs over to closed before locking their doors. A few of them waved at us with wide smiles on their faces, and I waved back without a thought in the world.

For the first time, I was being seen as a human being and not some royal subject who couldn't be approached. We passed through the small town and turned down a switchback trail leading further down to the beach. The petrichor scent of the water meeting the shores in the distance, infused with all the other delicious smells of the food and festivities, drifted through the crisp air.

All the people of this petite town had shown up with small carriages, creating little booths open for games like sack races and apple bobbing to the more creative booths with face paints and flower crowns. A little further up ahead was a giant outlined circle with heavy stones where men were throwing wood into the center of it, and then they lit it right before my eyes and it engulfed into a bright bonfire, lighting the entire area.

A small group of people was standing off to the side of the fire with instruments in hand, playing upbeat music as we passed by, parking the wagon. I realized that the wood Gavin had been chopping earlier was for the festival. The men that started the fire walked over, greeting Beth with wide smiles through their burly beards, slapping their hands on Wes and Beckett's backs, their way of greeting, as one man noticed Gavin stepping off of the wagon. As Gavin helped me down, the man dropped the wood and walked over, giving him a quick one-armed embrace.

"Ah! You're back, mate! Good to see you! We've missed ya!" The man was cheery with an accent from somewhere I didn't recognize, but it reminded me of Roland's which tugged a smile on my lips. He was wearing a long-sleeved tunic with some well-worn overalls. His belly pushed out some but I could tell the man was still in shape regardless of his fuller figure. He pointed to me.

"And who is this fine lass on your arm?" He winked at me playfully.

"Myla, meet Beau Hammett, the finest angler in all of Baela," Gavin said with a smile.

"Pleasure to me you, Beau."

"The pleasure is all mine, Miss Myla," he spoke kindly. "I'd love for you to meet my wife." On cue, a woman with warm brown skin walked up next to him with her textured tight black curls piled in ringlets atop her head. She was beautiful, her skin glowing in the firelight. Beau wrapped an arm around her waist.

"Hi, I'm Camella." She had a light smile and another accent I didn't recognize. Getting a closer look at her, she looked strangely familiar.

"Hi, nice to meet you. Oddly enough, you look like someone we know."

"That's probably because Camella and Beau are Roland's parents," Gavin chimed into the conversation.

"Speaking of Roland," Beau said, "where did that lad go?" Beau spoke in a natural loud tone.

"Go? Roland's here?" I asked with a shocked expression on my face.

"Yeah, he got in a few hours before the festival started, brought home his new fiancée."

"Harper?! Fiancée?" I exclaimed, huffing a breath of excitement.

"Yeah, that's the one. She's lovely," Camella responded.

"They told us how they spent a day searching the mountain pass for you both after you were separated and then stopped here before meeting you in Credia. When they didn't find you, they assumed that's where you would be headed."

"We will leave tonight for Credia," Gavin responded, giving my arm that was draped around his a light squeeze.

"They'll be here tonight," Camella said. "I'm sure they'll be happy to see you both." She glanced at her husband, gesturing to the festivities.

"Safe travels to you, mate! It's been good seeing you home." Beau slapped a heavy hand on Gavin's shoulder to bid him farewell as they walked away into the growing crowd.

"I see where Roland gets all his bustling personality." Gavin chuckled at my discovery. We walked toward the blazing fire, feeling the warmth of the flames sink into our skin against the cool evening air. The only light source was the fire as I tried to look out toward the ocean. I could hear the waves crashing in the distance and the smell of the salted water in the air. Jocelyn ran up to me, grabbing me by the hand.

"Myla! Myla! Will you dance with me?"

"Of course." Although I didn't think I had much of a choice considering she was already dragging me toward the crowded circle of people surrounding the sandy dance floor. "Where are your shoes?" I asked her, and she just giggled at me

"You don't need shoes to dance, silly!" She spun, and I kicked off my shoes and followed her lead. The cold, loose soil under my feet made me feel calmer in the moment's excitement. I looked back to Gavin, who was shaking his head with a smile stretching over his face as he watched us from the small crowd. Jocelyn pulled me into the center with a few other townspeople, twisting and twirling to the beat of the uplifting music. She danced and twirled along with them.

I did not know what I was doing, but I did my best to keep up with everyone else. I grabbed the bottom seam of my dress to kick out my feet, and Jocelyn did the same as we interlocked our arms while twisting around each other, giggling. More townspeople continued to join in, and before I knew it, we were surrounded by people cheering and dancing with smiles covering their faces.

Jocelyn got handed off to her brother, Wesley, but I didn't even see him get on the dance floor. When I looked at my surroundings, I saw Gavin grinning at me. My guess was at how ridiculous I must have looked, but I didn't care. I saw one of the townspeople walking through the crowd close to me with a tray full of drinks, and I grabbed a cup of ale and downed it in one go before I gathered the courage to dance alone in front of Gavin.

I held out my hand, asking him to dance, and he shook his head at me. Beau and a few other townspeople pushed him out into the dance circle.

"Get out there, my boy!" I heard Beau's thundering voice somewhere in the madness of the crowd, and then it happened. Something that I'd been waiting for. Gavin's hands intertwined with mine as we swung each other around the sandy floor. The wide smile on his face made my heart melt as our eyes locked. The world faded away except for the faint tune of the music in the background.

All of his features looked warmer, more relaxed, either from the light of the fire against him or because this truly was who Gavin was without the title of being my knight. As the song slowed, he pulled me against his muscled chest and my breath hitched, and not just from the fast-paced dancing. He held me close to him as we stepped slowly, more methodical than before.

"I thought you didn't dance," I murmured against his ear.

"I don't. But I have promises to keep." His whisper brushed my neck as he lowered his head, tucking it into the crook of my shoulder. His hot breath against my skin sent tingles down my spine as his arms tightened around me. My breath quickened, and I remembered we weren't alone, in some distant location. We were still in the center of the dance circle the townspeople created. Gavin pulled away, meeting my eyes.

"There is something I want to show you." He held out his hand and I took it without a second thought as he weaved his way through the crowd and out toward the open clearing up ahead just beyond the potluck. As we walked out toward the open land, the misty air coated my skin, cooling me from the heat of the crowded dance floor. Gavin took the lead down the path.

"Close your eyes," he commanded in a low seductive purr that made me shiver. I obliged as he led me. The land under my feet slowly changed from loose soil to more of a gritty powder-like substance under my bare feet. A smile tugged at my lips. It was something I'd never felt before. "Open your eyes." I did as he said, gasping at the view before me. I perched against the small ledge as the moonlight reflected a path along the calm waves of the water pushing and pulling against the shore below us.

The night sky was vividly beautiful, so clear I could see every darker part of the moon's surface as it loomed ahead so big I felt as if I could reach up and touch it. Millions of stars twinkled against the white round glow suspended above us. The waves were a jumble of blue glistening in the night. The gentle sounds of the waves lapping against the sand sounded like a lullaby.

I turned my head to the left, seeing Gavin leaning against one of the sandalwood trees, watching me intently. A smile curved one side of his mouth. Rubbing his thumb along his bottom lip, he looked down a moment before catching my eyes again.

"This is absolutely stunning," I spoke up, but his eyes never left mine.

"It is—breathtaking". The heated look in his gaze made my cheeks flush and mouth go dry.

"Gavin," I whispered, barely above the sound of the waves. Almost as if he could hear the want in my voice, his arms were wrapped around me within two strides. His eyes darkened right before his lips crashed against mine. My body ached for his touch. The bundle of nerves between my legs throbbed as my center pooled.

His mouth covered mine, a kiss full of passion, and I couldn't stop this want for Gavin, my knight. I wouldn't hold back for the man I had come to know and love. I wanted him—no, I needed him. I needed all of him. I pushed back enough to pull down the shoulders of my dress.

"Myla—" He said my name on a shaky breath.

"No, I want this. I want you, all of you." We shared the same breath.

"If I give you all of me, I'll never be able to walk away," he spoke with a deep purr.

"I'd never want you to." Our bodies clashed against one another like the waves against the shore, needing one another more than our bodies needed breath.

He pulled down my dress, revealing my peaked breasts. He took me in before peering back up at me, palming my face with his hands. He pulled me into another passionate kiss. My hands pulled up under his tunic. He broke our kiss long enough to let it slip over his head as he brought his lips back to mine. His hands slid down my back, ripping at the laced fitted back of my dress, letting it fall to my ankles, leaving me completely bare against the moonlit night.

Gavin drew me into him, nuzzled my shoulder while trailing kisses up my neck and nibbling against my ear as I undid his trousers. His desire pushed against them. He pulled his face back a moment, resting his forehead against mine. He gazed deeply into my eyes, searching my soul for approval, as if offering me one last plea to stop this before we went any further. But it was too late.

I had no control anymore. He was more important to me than any other thing in my life. I wanted him. My eyes gave him the answer he craved. He dragged his fingers lightly across my stomach, down to my heated core. His fingers slid into my wet opening. I was ready for him. The sensation of his touch made my knees go weak as he wrapped his other arm around me, holding my weight up as he plunged his fingers into me.

A moan escaped me as I let my head fall back with every thrust of his fingers. A wave of pleasure built within me as he found my small bundle of nerves, massaging it gently with his thumb. I wrapped my arms around his neck, arching myself further into his touch as he unraveled me. He swallowed my cries of pleasure with his lips. Pushing me back against a tree, he removed his fingers from me, trailing kisses down my chest. He cupped and squeezed my breasts as he went lower.

Kissing. Licking. Suckling.

He paused right above my throbbing core and it took everything in me not to arch against his lips. His tongue slid through me and I nearly came undone. Another moan escaped me as he took one of my legs, resting it on his shoulder to get better access. His tongue was relentless as he circled my nub, and entered me again with his fingers. The wave of pleasure crested and exploded through me, sending a burst of tingling to my limbs.

He followed my lead as I pulled him to the ground. I straddled him, and seeing his need pushing against his trousers only made me want more. I hastily pulled at his belt, releasing his hardened length. Gavin flipped me over gently, hovering above me, holding himself up with one arm. He ran his calloused hand along my side, he paused everything, meeting my eyes.

"I want all of you," I said as my eyes trailed down his body, worried he may stop. I took in the sight of him.

"And I want you to have all of me." At the moment the words left his lips, he refused to hold back any longer. He gently inched inside of me, holding my hooded gaze before his lips trailed down my neck again as he moved in deeper, harder. His hum of pleasure made a shiver skate down my spine.

I arched my back, feeling the need building in my core once more for him as we slowly rocked against each other's movements. My fingers tangled in his hair as my arms tightened around his neck. His hand trailed down my body, making me shudder and buck against him harder—faster. Our bodies moved like a demented rhythm filled with needy passion. He let out a graveled groan, making me fall over the edge of my release.

I felt him pulse within me as he let go of his, making my core clench around him. Gavin rolled his hips against mine until every little sound faded to nothing but deep gasping breaths. He moved to his side, looping his arms around me as I rested my head against his chest and gazed up at the stars. He placed a light kiss against my temple as we lay there with nothing but the lullaby of the ocean in the distance and the glistening stars above.

I lost track of the time, still feeling the euphoria of the moments before. Propping myself up on my elbow, I faced him and he turned his head toward me.

"I want to get a closer look. Would you walk with me?"

"Myla, I'd go anywhere with you," he said with a grin that made the finches fly into my chest. Gavin stood and held out his hand to help me up as he pulled me into him for one last kiss. I kissed him back through the smile plastered on my face. I couldn't help the joy coursing through me.

"Do you mean that?" I asked as he stepped back to pull up his trousers while I fetched my dress and quickly threw it back on.

"Of course, anywhere." He spoke without a doubt. When I turned back to him, he was dressed and waiting for me. He looped one of his arms around my waist and I did the same.

"Run away with me?" I asked, looking away, nervous about his response as we walked down to the sandy shores below. The sand grew softer the closer we got to the water, and my nerves grew with every step we took forward. Gavin paused and pulled me into him. He palmed my face as he brought his forehead to mine.

"Yes," he whispered, and the burn of tears stirred behind my eyes as he gently thumbed my cheeks. My emotions overflowed from my chest as my shoulders slacked from the relief of his admission. He would run with me. We could be together—we were together. My smile beamed as he put his lips to mine again.

A single tear escaped me in my bliss as everything I had ever dreamed of played out in front of me. Gavin pulled away, wiped my tear, and wrapped his arm around me as we continued down to the water's edge. If there wasn't such a chill tonight, I'd go swimming out there. I plopped my rear on the ground just a few feet from where the water rose, shoving my toes into the coarse, moist sand. The small shimmers of starlight reflecting along the great expanse of water took my breath away. The smell, this place, all reminded me of one thing—one person. Maybe that was why I loved it so much? Had it been because I had been in love with Gavin this entire time?

I had been so preoccupied that I hadn't eaten, and my stomach reminded me with its loud grumbling. The smell of the festival foods lightly swishing through the breeze was making it worse. Gavin chuckled next to me.

"Myla, the ocean isn't going anywhere. We can go grab a bite."

"I don't want to leave. I've waited my whole life for this view, but if you want to be ever so kind as to go grab all this lovely food I've been hearing about since riding into town with you and bring it down here for us to enjoy on this beautiful beach together, I wouldn't be opposed." I winked at him with a smile. He smiled, but it didn't last long. His features tugged down some, turning into a more worrisome expression.

"Myla, I don't want to leave you alone."

"Gavin, it's fine. Go, I can take care of myself." I gave him a one-sided grin.

"You're sure?"

"Yes, I will stay in this spot until you return," I spoke while bringing my arms up and around my knees, dragging them up to my chest. The flutter of nerves returned to my stomach, fighting against my racing thoughts. I wanted to tell Gavin what he meant to me, that I loved him, but I pushed down those urges. I decided I would do it once he came back.

"Okay, I'll be right back. Don't move," he said while giving me a quick kiss on the head. "Here, take this." He handed me the same dagger from before. "You know what to do with it, just in case."

"You worry too much," I said, taking it from his grasp.

"No such thing, love," he said with a grin and a wink before turning away. Gods that smile.

Love...

Did he feel the same? After his footsteps receded so far that I couldn't hear them anymore, I squealed silently to myself. I didn't know what to do about Credia, Baela, or my father, but I took in the sight before me, not wanting to let any of those things steal my happiness. A few moments passed before I heard a twig snap close by behind me.

"That was fast," I said before a strong-muscled arm wrapped around my shoulders from behind, hauling me to my feet. The stranger behind me used his other hand to silence my scream by shoving a damp cloth in my mouth that had a strong, bitter smell clinging to it. Everything slowed down, making my vision go fuzzy.

With the last of my strength, I shoved the dagger into the man's thigh, making him release me with a grunt of pain, throwing me down into the sand, hard. I yanked the cloth out of my mouth and crawled away before he kicked me in my side. The pain shot through me, the force knocking me over, sending me sliding into the wet sand. The water seeping into my dress felt warm against my prickling skin. That was when I knew something was wrong. It was late fall, almost winter, and the water would be freezing.

Whatever was on the cloth was affecting my vision. It was fading slowly to the sound of not just one, but two male voices surrounding me. Although I couldn't place where they were coming from. The pain in my side didn't feel like pain anymore, more like a faint tingling sensation that made my limbs feel heavy, and my eyes rolled back as I drifted into unconsciousness.

Chapter Twenty-Three

GAVIN

Trudging back up the switchback trail from the beach still had my whole body buzzing with emotion. It almost didn't seem real. Myla wanted to be with me just as much as I wanted her, and it made something awaken in me for the first time in a long while. Being a knight amid war for all those years taught me to put a hold on any desires or feelings I had and to lock them away.

Our job, our duty was then to the kingdom and the royals we were supposed to protect and nothing more. But from the moment I laid eyes on Myla, I had been drawn to her, and I had never felt this way about anyone before. She gave herself to me, and me to her, and there was no way I'd be able to watch her marry another man after tonight.

I walked past the large dance circle with the blazing bonfire, down the path full of carriages and makeshift stands on either side, noting the food and games. I saw Jocelyn and my brothers Bennett and Wesley bobbing for apples a few paces away, and it warmed my heart to catch them with smiles on their faces. While distracted, a heavy hand landed on my shoulder, pulling me into an embrace, and when I turned to see who it was, it was Roland. I returned his one-handed hug with a few pats on the back.

Harper stood behind him.

"Gods, Gavin! Where did you guys end up? We looked everywhere for you," Roland said.

"We came into town instead of taking the mountain pass." I looked away a moment, holding the guilt of not returning sooner, but he pulled me back into a soft shouldered hug.

"I'm proud of you."

"Thank you." He nodded as he recognized my knowing expression. He had kept in contact with my family for me when I wasn't capable of doing it for myself. Harper cut in.

"Where's Myla?"

"She's back at the beach. I'm grabbing some food and then heading back down there."

"I have to show her! I'll see you both down there." She squealed excitedly, showing me her ring before dabbing a quick kiss on

Roland's cheek and skipping away. Roland walked next to me, strolling up to a stand serving food.

"What can I getcha?" the man asked with a smile.

"Do you want anything?" I asked Roland, but he shook his head. "Harper and I grabbed something already."

"Surprise me with your best," I spoke to the server.

"Coming right up!" His voice was loud and cheerful, tugging a smile on my lips. I had missed home.

"So, what happened between you and Myla?" Roland asked with a satisfactory grin plastered on his face.

"Is it that obvious?" I asked.

"Yes, I've never seen you this relaxed, or what's the word the ladies use? Glowing," he said the last word on the end of a chuckle, mocking a girly accent, and I couldn't help my laugh, but it soon faded.

"I don't know what to do, Roland. I'm in love with her and I can't let her marry another man now—I won't."

"I wish I knew what to tell you, but you're a churl in hot water now."

"Thanks for the confidence," I huffed.

"I'll be here whatever happens, mate," Roland assured me as the older man handed me my food. We started walking back down in the beach's direction when I heard someone yelling in the distance, and then I realized who it was. Harper held my bloodied dagger, running toward us with her eyes filled with tears and panic. For a moment, the world crashed around me. The food fell to the ground and my heart sank to the lowest pits of my stomach.

"She's gone," is all Harper said.

She was gone. They took her. Either King Henry or Prince Wyatt, but either way, I had to get her back. My vision tunneled. My only goal was to leave now. They couldn't have gotten too far in such a short time. I turned to search past the bonfire for the wagon we came on, but it was gone. I looked back toward the games that my siblings were at and, after finding them in the crowd, I ran to them.

"Beckett, where's Mother?"

"She went back home. We told her we'd stay here with Jocelyn for a while longer and then walk home," he said, glancing over to Wesley and Jocelyn with a worried expression growing on his face. "Is something wrong, brother?"

"Myla was taken." I spoke in a hushed tone so Wesley and Jocelyn couldn't hear me. I placed a hand on his shoulder. "Keep your eyes and ears open." He gave me a nod of acknowledgment as I rushed past. He grabbed the crook of my arm, halting me.

"Hey, be careful." I tried to nod and pull away but he nudged me back again. "And come back home this time."

"I'll do my best." And that was the last thing I said before turning to Harper.

"Stay here. You're Myla's servant. They may be after you too." I started sprinting to the house with Roland and Harper right on my heels.

"I'm not staying behind," Harper exclaimed.

"None of us are," Roland said, and I accepted the comfort of their support, but the fear grew just beneath of what was to come while trying to get Myla back.

Upon approaching my childhood home, the shattering sound of glass breaking caught my attention, and I motioned for Roland and Harper to go around the back. Harper handed my dagger back to me and followed Roland, crouching low to avoid the small windows along the front of my home. I brought my head up to peer inside, and what I met made me lose my logical way of thinking.

My mother was strewn up by knights of Baela as they ransacked the house. All the dishes and silverware were shattered and thrown about in the kitchen. The furniture had been flipped and sliced open with swords aimlessly. It took every fiber in my being to assess the situation before busting down the door.

There seemed to be two of them wandering around the small living area about to head up the stairs. I waited until I could no longer see their feet as they climbed up the stairwell. I glanced at my mother, and her eyes widened when she noticed me. She shook her head, motioning me to run, but I would not leave her.

I opened the front door as quietly as I could before rushing to her, grabbing for the ropes tied at her wrists. She squirmed, shaking her head and crying out as I tried to cut her free, but it was too late. The searing pain on the back of my head throbbed as I overheard a familiar guttural voice.

"You missed one." I rolled over onto my back to meet him but got struck again with a kick to my ribs as the other two knights came back downstairs. My mother's hushed screams echoed around the room through the cloth gag wrapped around her head. I glanced toward the back door, seeing Roland peeking around the corner, and I gave him a dismissive eye with a small shake of my head, acting as if I was shaking off the pain of the blow. I warned them to stay away. One of the unknown knights kicked my dagger away from me and pulled me up onto my knees by the hair. My bruised ribs barked in pain as I sat upright, meeting the man I hated as much as King Henry: Fredrick. The King's royal puppet. He was wearing a full set of royal armor that caught me off guard. I had never seen him in fighting leathers, let alone armor. Who all did King Henry send to find us?

"What do you want?" I snarled.

"Well, that's a silly question, don't you think, sir... Oh, what was it again, Gabe?"

"Gavin," I growled, clenching my jaw so tight my teeth ached.

"Today is your lucky day, Sir Gavin." He said my name in his haughty tone while leaning down to study me.

"Why's that?"

"Because you're wanted alive." He cocked his arm back and landed a hard punch to my face. I spat my blood at his feet, splattering his shined, unworn armor, and he cocked his arm back and hit me again. I leaned forward as far as I could against the pull of the man's hand gripped in my hair and the others restraining my arms. I looked Fredrick in the eyes, this time tasting the tang of blood dripping from my mouth before I spoke.

"May whatever god you serve have mercy on you, cause when I get a hold of you, I won't." One side of Fredrick's mouth curved into a grin.

"I'm sure," was all I received before I met the ringing in my ears and the pain throbbing against the back of my head once more. My vision faded to black.

Chapter Twenty-Four

MYLA

I didn't know if it had been days or hours since I was on the beach. They covered my head with a burlap sack. My wrists, ankles, and neck were raw from the ropes binding them. My stomach stopped roaring with hunger and had turned into an empty ache in my center as if it had accepted my fate just as much as I had. I knew whoever had taken me was on the move. Every movement of the wooden wagon shoved small splinters through my dress and into my skin. When the wagon finally jolted to a stop, the wagon door flopped down with a thud before a sizeable set of icy hands grabbed my ankles, dragging me out of the back.

He used something sharp to cut the ropes from my feet so I could walk on my own.

He yanked my arm and hauled me to my feet while half dragging me down a path full of jagged cold rocks. My bare feet burned not only from the pain, but from the chill outside. It must still be night? Or had it already been a full day from when I was taken?

My captor dragged me along until the fog in my mind slowly cleared. The loose gravel shifted under my feet, causing me to stumble. My captor didn't care, dragging me on until I gathered myself upright again. After what felt like walking this long path forever, the ground changed to a solid, smooth surface while the warmth of the room I had walked into knocked the chill off my bones. The man holding my arms shoved me to the ground as a door thudded closed behind us. I didn't fight as I heard footsteps drawing closer from the echo of the building. A familiar voice sounded.

"What happened to your leg?"

"She was a bit handsy, Your Majesty," my captor responded.

Wyatt. I was in Credia in Prince Wyatt's castle being delivered to him like an insignificant piece of property. I lay there still as I wrapped my head around everything happening. All I could think about was if Gavin was okay, or what he must think about me disappearing. Was he looking for me? Was he safe? I did my best to swallow the emotional rock growing in my throat. Wyatt snapped his fingers as he spoke again.

"Tend to her. I don't want to see her like this, make her look marvelous," he said as his footsteps receded and two sets of gentle, warm hands helped me up on either side of me to escort me through a castle I had never been to before. The smell of sweet cinnamon and butter wafted through the air, making me assume we were passing the kitchen during breakfast. I had been in that wagon a full day. I did my best to focus on how many paces we were moving in every direction. Being unable to see made it impossible. After going up two sets of stairs, one being straight and narrow and the other being a spiral, I suspected I was in one of the towers.

How we got to the tower, I didn't know. I felt like we went through a small maze before making it this far. How was I going to escape without getting caught? This wasn't like home, where I recognized my surroundings and could sneak out in guard leathers.

The servants sat me down in a room filled with warm steam, smelling of wildflowers and lavender. A bathing chamber, I presumed. One of them untied my wrists while the other worked on the rope tied around my neck. As they slipped off, the server took the burlap sack off my head and I could finally see again. One servant saw the fear on my face because she tried to comfort me.

"Madam, we have orders to tend to you. I'm going to undress you now, okay?" She spoke quaintly while placing a gentle hand on my shoulder. All I could do was nod at her while fiddling with my hands on my lap. "Can you stand up for me?" she asked, and I complied, standing on sore feet. Now that my body was relaxing, all the aches and pains from the abuse and travel came to the surface. Everything hurt, even breathing.

The servants took down my dress and slowly revealed all the cuts and bruises from the last day. Whatever was on that cloth had to have been strong to knock me out for so long. One servant inspected the biggest bruise covering my ribs from where the knight kicked me. She ran her fingers over it, making me flinch in pain.

"I'm sorry," she murmured, "just wanting to make sure nothing's broken."

"What's your names?" I asked, glancing between them both. They looked up at me, dumbfounded that I cared to know their names at all.

"I'm Lucille, Your Highness." The one inspecting my side spoke first. She reminded me of Harper a little with her auburn hair and pasty skin, but Harper's hair was more red than brown and she had a darker complexion.

"I'm Ana, Your Highness," the other said, and she stood to give me a small curtsy. She had warm brown eyes with short, loosely curled blonde hair framing her face full of light freckles. Lucille looked at Ana and realized she hadn't bowed, so she hastily stood to bow with Ana. I touched both of their arms gently, stopping their actions.

"That's unnecessary. I'm Myla, and you can call me Myla." They both looked at my comforting touch on their arms and gave me subtle smiles as both of their shoulders sagged a little. They seemed more relaxed being in the same room as a royal.

"You aren't like the other royals, are you?" Ana said, almost as if it weren't a question but more of a statement.

"I would think not," I said as a warm smile pulled across my features.

"Come now, let's get you taken care of, my lady." Lucille helped me get to my feet, guiding me to the tub steaming to the brim with hot water. I sank into it. The burn against all my cuts and bruises made me wince, but the warmth of the bath soaking into my skin was amazing with the slicing chill of winter still in my bones.

Lucille stayed with me while Ana left to tend to other matters. She gently massaged her fingers through my hair, doing her best not to pull at the matted parts from the ride here. I lathered myself the best I could and rinsed as she grabbed a comb to take care of the tangles.

"I don't mean to pry, my lady, but the castle has been tense the last couple of days awaiting your arrival. Especially after the King's death. What happened out there?" she asked, and I swallowed my surprise. I knew the King had been sick, but I didn't know about his passing.

Once again, she reminded me of Harper by how straightforward she was with her prying questions. She was strong and confident. Unafraid. Or at least, that was what Harper had always portrayed to me through our friendship. She was always the confident one. The one that asked the questions and knew how to get what she wanted. Lucille reminded me of that. She had that same fire in her heart. I could see it.

God, I missed Harper. Was that why I noticed so many similarities between them? Was I trying to kid myself? Surely that wasn't the case.

"Prince Wyatt had me hunted and brought to him because my timeline wasn't to his liking," I replied with a bite in my tone.

"He's never been a man with much patience," she said, brushing out the last of the knots in my hair. "Was it because of the knight?" Her question caught me off guard. How did she know about Gavin? It was almost as if she could read my thoughts. "I've heard the rumors," she murmured, rinsing my hair one last time, grabbing the towel and holding it up so I could step out with some coverage as she wrapped it around me. Every step sent aches up my sore legs. My silence answered her question for her.

"Can you dress yourself? Or would you like my assistance?" she asked kindly, noticing my wince.

"I'm okay, Lucille. Thank you." She walked out, shutting the door gently behind her, and I turned to look at myself in the mirror. My left side was splotched with dark purples and blues from where the knight kicked me, and minor cuts were randomly placed all over my body from the rough journey here, but I'd live.

Having dressed, I pulled my damp hair back into a braid, leaving out some strands to frame my face. The dress was long and fit loosely, and I discarded the corset for the sake of my side and because I rather enjoyed being able to breathe air. I placed a pair of comfortable flats on my feet before standing and taking one last look in the mirror.

I saw where my lip busted at some point through the scuffle, and the circles under my eyes were more shadowed than normal from the lack of rest. Again, I'd live. I ran my hands down the dress one last time, straightening myself before stepping out of the bathing chamber. I glanced around the room they had given me, and it reminded me a lot of the room from Baela. It made me wonder if Wyatt did it on purpose to butter me up.

The ceiling reached grand heights and was filled with whimsy, dusted gold designs against the pearl-white walls filled with gold-framed artwork. The balcony French door windows had unique designs compared to the ones back home, but the balcony was still in the same place. Long wine-red curtains framed the doorway that differed from the blue ones in Baela, but those were the only differences. It was soulless. It made me miss Gavin's family home filled with the sweet smells of Beth's cooking, the sounds of Jocelyn's laughter as she played with her elder brothers, and the cozy, quaint living space warmed by the fireplace. This room was too large, too silent—too dead. There was no love here.

This room was where dreams of living a simpler life ran to die. They slipped away from me the longer I stood gawking at my surroundings, wishing they would change back into that small farmhouse by the beach I had grown to love in the short time I'd been there.

"Myla?" I gave myself a mental shake at the sound of my name on Lucille's lips.

"Hmm?" was all I mustered to say while looking in her direction with dead eyes.

"Prince Wyatt has called for you."

"Right." I straightened my spine and put on the mask of the obedient princess. I fell right back into the shell that I had tried so hard to climb out of. Lucille stepped in line in front of me, leading me to wherever Prince Wyatt was.

We moved down a few hallways that were wide enough for two lanes of horses and carriages before we took one final left into a grand throne room. Wyatt perched on the oversized red velvet seat rimmed with intertwining gold lace designs that almost extended to the ceilings. A small seat sat right next to it. It was plain. Had the same red velvet cushions but was a step lower than the other with fewer details surrounding it.

"Myla." He drew out my name with his boasting tone like a snake's hiss as he held out his hands, gesturing to the surrounding room. "Please, come here, love." He gave me a fake smile that didn't meet his eyes. The whole situation made my body stiffen.

He didn't wait for me to walk toward him. He strode toward me, wrapping both his arms around my hips, drawing me into him. I placed my arms in front of myself to create some space between us, but it did nothing. He leaned down, bringing one hand up to cup my face while pulling me into his open-mouthed kiss. My insides quivered with disgust. He pulled me back, holding me by my elbows in place.

"I've missed you." He interlaced one of my arms with his while walking me to the thrones and sitting me down on the small one. "I have a surprise for you." His voice was as cold as ice as he sat next to me. The tone of his voice made my face go ashen, and my heart sunk into the pits of my stomach. What had he done? Or, more importantly, who had he hurt? "Come forth," he called from across the room.

Two knights came bursting through the side doors on the right, dragging a body between the two of them with a sack roped around the head with arms and feet bound. My body trembled. The two men stood in front of the steps to the throne while tossing the person to the ground with an echoing thud, and I looked away a moment from the fear building within me.

"Remove the sack and show my bride..." He paused, looking at me with a wicked grin. "...her surprise." I could feel the burn building behind my eyes as the rock formed in my throat. The knights ripped the sack off and I saw him: Gavin. He was beaten and bloodied, barely able to keep his eyes open from how swollen they were. They had beaten him, and seeing the mess of injuries and pain creased on his face as he tried to look up at me made searing tears fall from my eyes. I stood to go to him.

"Sit. Down," was all Wyatt said when he saw me jump to my feet.

"Myla—" Gavin tried to speak, but my name came out as a raspy whisper.

"Do not speak unless you are spoken to." As Wyatt spoke, one guard turned and pulled his arm back to punish Gavin some more, but I couldn't—no, I wouldn't stand idly by while they killed the man I loved.

"No!" I shouted as I fell to the floor in front of Gavin, blocking him from harm's way. I turned to Wyatt as he stared daggers at Gavin. "Wyatt, listen to me." My voice trembled so hard I didn't sound like myself. "If you kill him, I will spend the rest of my life fleeing and fighting you every step of the way." Now he turned his gaze to me with his eyes filled with venom. "But, if you let him go, let him live, I'll do whatever you want." My lip trembled again as I nodded to Wyatt. "I'll marry you, I won't run or hide, and I'll give you an heir if that is what you wish, just let him live, let him go." I crawled up the steps on my knees before Wyatt, placing my hands on his knees. "Please," I begged with eyes filled with tears.

"Myla—don't do this..." Gavin spoke, his words filled with agony.

"Prove it or he dies where he sits," Wyatt spoke, peering down at me from his throne. I ignored my body's every urge to get as far away from this man as possible. I kissed him. He opened his mouth for me and I deepened our kiss as our tongues slid over one another's. He leaned forward, pulling me closer, and I felt his desire harden against my chest as I remained on my knees in front of him.

He tasted of mint and stale tobacco. It took everything in me to fight the urge to pull away from his touch as I waited for him to end the kiss. He drew back, looking at me with hooded eyes. He placed his hand in mine and helped me stand.

"Release him," Wyatt commanded, and the knights hauled him to his feet.

"Wait," I pleaded, glancing at Gavin and then back to Wyatt. "Could I have a moment, please?" He looked as if he were about to turn me down so I added, "What's a moment when we have a lifetime together, darling?" I smothered my words in sweet warmth. Wyatt gave me a side smile.

"Fine, but just a moment." I nodded, giving him a smile as he released my hand and walked toward the door, dismissing the knights with him. I didn't move until I heard the door shudder to a close.

Chapter Twenty-Five

Gavin

Myla gave up everything for my life. If the tables were turned, I'd be the one to make the sacrifice. I didn't want this for her. In the middle of my thoughts, her warm hands cupped my face, bringing me back to reality. The pain pulsed in my head from the brutality of the beatings. I ached from every limb. They must have continued to beat me after I had passed out. Oh gods, my mother, was she alright? What did they do to her?

Everything was too much. My eyes began burning, not from the pain of the physical wounds, but from the emotional ones. My family, Myla, and Roland were all doing everything they could for me, and yet here I was, on my knees, covered in my blood as the tears streaked my face.

I heard Myla's voice slowly echoing louder and louder as it grew closer and closer, but she was already here. Her arms wrapped around my shoulders as my head rested in the crook of her arm.

"Gavin, please... can you hear me?" The fear in her tone made me fully come to my senses.

"Myla, you can't do this."

"I already did." Tears swelled in her eyes. "One of us has to get out of this mess and live. I always knew it would be you." Her voice cracked, but she smiled at me with eyes filled with love. "Thank you for making the best of the time we had."

I wrapped my arms around her, pulling her into my chest. Her scent engulfed me and I reveled in it like it was my last breath. The thought of losing Myla forever knocked me harder than any blow I had ever taken and cut deeper than any sword I had ever crossed. She pulled away from me, and I cupped her face in my hands, bringing her forehead to mine.

"You. You were my wish." Her brow furrowed before she realized what I meant.

"And you were mine." Tears free fell as she gave me a sad smile.

"I will come back for you, I promise."

"Gavin, don't. Get out of here and live out your life. We'll meet again in the next one."

"My life wouldn't be worth living without you in it." I kissed her with sore lips, tasting the salt of our tears and the tang of my blood. My chest tightened; the war of the love I had for this woman and the determination to keep her charged through my chest. I would get her back. I swore it. The doors swept open, and the knights stormed in once again with Prince Wyatt right behind them.

Myla jerked away, taking a few steps back as they grabbed me and escorted me out of the room. I peered over my shoulder and saw Myla go rigid as Prince Wyatt put his arm around her. She straightened her dress while holding her hands in front of herself to stay still, but the dread was written all over her face.

I had to get her out of here. I stumbled along as the knights dragged me out of the throne room. They quickly trudged me through the royal yard and to the graveled front gates. I did my best to take in my surroundings, but with the sun high in the sky and my vision adjusting to the light of day considering my injuries, I got little to go off of.

The knights threw me to the ground, one spitting near me before they closed the gates, glaring at me with hateful eyes while I got to my feet and they locked them. The clunk of the gate being secured felt like the stamp on Myla's fate, but I refused to accept it. I would change our fates whether or not we had to spend the rest of our lives running from royalty. Anything would be better than this.

I limped down the gravel trail, my clothes tattered and stained with blood. I needed a horse. At this rate, I wouldn't make it back to my family for days with my leg the way it was. I didn't think it was broken, but every step was a chore. It was sprained, but I couldn't stop moving. Every hour, every minute, was time that Myla had to be with that egotistical prince. I didn't know what I'd do if he touched her. Forced her into something she didn't want to do because of me. To save my life. I shook away the thought and tried to focus on the task at hand: getting her back.

I wasn't sure what path to take to get back to my hometown, but it wasn't the mountains. Both were dangerous, and if I got attacked by wolves, I wouldn't make it on this leg. I pushed myself forward through the aches and pains into the woods up ahead. The deadened trees made the trail look more ominous now that all the leaves had fallen off for the winter.

Every ragged breath made my lungs feel as if they were collapsing in on themselves. I leaned against a large trunk to keep myself upright. The snap of a twig turned my attention behind me. My heartbeat pounded, and my breath quickened. Grabbing a large stick from the ground, I hauled it back, preparing myself for the worst. I stepped forward carefully. My eyes scoured the surroundings more than once.

I turned to my left and swung the stick with full force, knocking the man to the ground. I pulled it back again, preparing to land another blow, but then I saw who it was. Roland. He stood, grabbed the stick from my hands, and chucked it.

"I come to your rescue and this is how you repay your knight in shining armor?" He clapped a hand down on my forearm, nearly taking me to the ground with my weak leg as I helped him up. "That's just rude."

I managed a smile at him, "I didn't know it was you."

"Oh, yeah, sure." He threw a dismissive hand in the air. "Come on, we have to go."

"How did you know I was here?" I asked. My eyes widened when I remembered he was at the house when I was taken.

"My mother!?"

"She's safe; everyone is safe. They only took you," he reassured me.

"Oh, thank god." I blew out a shaky breath.

"Harper and I have been camped near here, keeping a close watch on the knights' rounds. When I saw them dragging you out, I thought the worst. I came down to save you, but then they just let you go."

I looked down, feeling the pain of Myla's sacrifice all over again.

"Myla willingly gave herself to Wyatt to save my life." I peered back up to Roland, giving him a knowing look, and he shook his head.

"You have that wild look in your eye, mate. Let me guess... you're about to do something rash." I didn't answer; I didn't need to. I wanted to keep moving. I draped my arm over his shoulder, relieving some of my weight from my bad leg. He helped me move along back to their camp, where Harper was waiting for us. I sat on a pack lying on the ground hard with a grunt, wincing while

Roland and Harper looked me over. Harper wrapped my ankle while Roland grabbed me some water.

"Thank you," I murmured to her, but she gave me an eye roll. Typical Harp.

"Did you tell her how you felt?" she questioned, continuing to give me the stink eye.

"Not fully...," I huffed.

"Still stupid," she whispered while trying to be gentle with my ankle. "The smartest thing you've done," she continued while finishing up the wrap, "is deciding to save her from that place." She smirked before getting back to her feet as Roland handed me a skin of water. Harper grabbed a bag and pulled out some dried meats and cheeses, and I realized how starved I was, taking it from her before she could even get it out of the bag. Roland cackled at me, acting like a cave dweller.

I chomped down on the stiff beef before shoving a slice of cheese into my mouth. All of it tasted like peppered firewood, but it was something to eat. I washed down the food, drinking the full skin of water in almost one go. My mouth was so dry, but after the food and water, I felt myself pulling from the dizzy state I was in before.

"So what's the plan?" Roland asked.

"I'm going to get her back."

"We're going to get her back." They spoke up almost in unison with one another, and for the first time since I lost Myla, I smiled.

Chapter Twenty-Six

Myla

I confused the days with the nights. I barely got out of bed. Lucille and Ana opening my curtains in the mornings was the only reason I ever saw the light of day. Not because I was trapped in this room, particularly, but because I had nothing left. I had gotten little to no sleep through my time in Credia, although my bed was where I had stayed.

I had barely stomached enough food to remain living. I traded a castle of physical wounds for a castle of emotional ones, and I couldn't decide which was worse. At least physical wounds healed after a few days. The emotional ones I had to live with for the rest of my life. But this morning was different. I had to drown out my sorrows and get up. Because today was my wedding day. The only thing keeping me from leaping off my balcony and ending it all was the warm comfort of knowing Gavin was alive and free. My sacrifice wasn't for nothing.

Lucille and Ana had been a godsend. They had done their utmost best to make me feel better over the last couple of weeks since I saw Gavin being dragged out of the throne room. I wished I could have shielded him from witnessing me kiss that disgusting excuse of a man. I huffed a breath at the thought, and Ana and Lucille looked in my direction as they whisked around my room, preparing gowns and jewels expensive enough to bring towns out of poverty.

It made me sick. How could any human in this world see struggling families and act as if they had no means of helping? Not even the slightest. I thought my father was a monster, stingy with his coin, but Prince Wyatt was a bigger beast with his riches than even my father, something I didn't think was possible.

Lucille and Ana had told me the rumors of Credia's deprived state of townspeople, same as Baela. It added one more thing to the list of why I hated royalty. Luckily, I didn't have to face Wyatt much this last week, other than the ridiculous brunch he made me attend every day. The way he looked at me across the table with his lewd eyes made me want to gag at the thoughts of us he had swimming in that colossal head of his.

Knowing that those same sentiments would soon be my reality after our wedding today made my whole body cringe at the thought of his hands on me. Maybe I could get out of it. Considering how persistent Wyatt was, that was doubtful.

I believed the only reason he wasn't constantly around now was because he knew he got what he wanted: me. Him stalking me from a distance like prey in the days leading up to our wedding was fun for him. Every glance, every unwanted touch, the anticipation of him knowing he would have me made the dread within me grow every passing day. Until today, the day it consumed me. He enjoyed the hunt, knowing he had already won. And there was nothing I could do about it.

I stepped up onto the pedestal in front of the trifold mirrors where Ana and Lucille instructed me to go. Like a numb vessel, I obeyed and nodded with whatever they asked. They had put me in an extravagant wedding gown more for a queen than a princess, likely what Prince Wyatt had chosen for me to wear today.

Although it was beautiful, the person wearing it wasn't. Peering at myself in the glass, my eyes were gray and as cold as the castle's stone walls. I was thin, thinner than I had been in a long time. The lack of motivation to even get up out of bed to eat would be the culprit behind my thinned figure and the dark sunken circles around my eyes.

Studying myself, the knot rose in my throat as my eyes burned with the tears building behind them. I hadn't cried since the last time I saw Gavin. I lay in my misery until now. Held everything inside. But seeing myself in this wedding dress made my nightmares shift into a reality, and I didn't know how to stop the turmoil clawing inside me.

I couldn't get enough air into my lungs. The room was small, too small, reflecting at me through the glass. It caved in around me. My heart hammered wildly, my body shuddered, and my knees gave out from under me. A warm embrace from either side was enough to make me completely crumble. Tears streamed down my face as I wrapped my arms around myself and squeezed. Soft sobs escaped me as I released days' worth of pent up despair.

Lucille and Ana held me and rocked me gently on the hard floor. I made no attempt at hiding my tears or wiping them away as my hands slid loosely back into my lap. My breathing became more even, and Lucille moved in front of me, lifting my head and wiping my tears.

"My lady." Her voice was a soothing song. "I know that this is hard, but we're here for you." My vision slowly cleared. Lucille's features softened with a reassuring smile, reminding me I wasn't alone, no matter how much I felt like I was. "Come on, let's get you cleaned up." Ana walked over with a cool wet rag to wipe my face.

At least they hadn't done my makeup yet. Then I'd look even worse than I already did, if that was even possible. Lucille didn't ask me to move. She asked nothing more of me than what I had to give, and at this point, that was simply my presence. She cleaned up my face while Ana brought over the jewels and makeup. They worked together, showering me with jewels and painting my face, lastly adding a tiara to my head. The next time I peered into the mirror, I looked like a goddess of wealth.

Taking in a shaky breath, I kept myself calm. Stepping over to the balcony windows, I met the array of dresses and suits of the finest silks, all royals who traveled here for the wedding. I knew the time was coming. Lucille and Ana stood there patiently waiting until I was ready to make the walk down to the courtyard where all the guests were waiting. I put on my emotionless mask, straightened my back, and sauntered to the doors while Ana and Lucille matched my stride on either side of me.

My steps were slow, but even. Anything to slow down the reality of what was about to happen. Each step I took down the stairwell was a step closer to the hell awaiting me at the end of the aisle. The grand foyer opened up to the courtyard, but none of the guests could see me yet. A woman came in through the doors, rushing toward me, her dress snug on her every curve, shimmering with the swish of her hips.

"Oh, thank heavens you're here." She waved her hand forward for me to come along with her, and Ana and Lucille gave me a nod of encouragement before the lady in red practically yanked me outside. We stood behind the tall hedges, knights placed in every corner.

"Are you ready?" she asked me with a beaming smile, and I just nodded. She moved to the arched opening between the long hedges, waving to the musicians to start the bridal music. The voices on the other side of the green wall slowly settled into whispers before they went completely silent until all I heard was the gentle music.

Closing my eyes, taking one last deep breath before I opened them, perfectly placing my mask of stone back on my face, I turned the corner, and all eyes whipped toward me. Some whispered, and others gave me awkward smiles. I looked at Wyatt, who was dressed in his finest silk suit of black and gold, with a sword hanging from his side.

I paused a moment, stopping where I stood, taking in the sight. I wasn't sure if it was out of pure horror or if it was because my feet refused to let me go any further. Flowers cascaded on either side of the aisle while Wyatt stood under an arch filled with blooming white roses. I glanced through the crowd, not seeing my father, but I caught eyes with who he sent in his place.

Fredrick granted me a smug smile before I gave myself a mental shake and forced my legs to take another step forward, and then another, and another until I was standing in front of Wyatt. He was taking my hands into his with his cocky arrogance radiating from every pore. An old man stood up from beside us, who I presumed was the priest to marry us, and it made my stomach twist into knots. I couldn't believe I was actually doing this. This was really happening.

I focused my eyes straight ahead, fixated on the rose pinned onto Wyatt's suit, knowing that if I met his gaze, I might break down again. The old man began, his voice croaky.

"Dearly beloved, we are gathered here today to celebrate the matrimony of Prince Wyatt Stagwhind of Credia and Princess Myla Elouise Blake of Baela." He paused, looking up from his book toward Wyatt with his raspy elder tone. "If any are in objection to this, please speak here and now or forever hold your peace." There was a beat of tensed silence, and I held my breath, but I kept myself grounded on the rose to keep myself steady. The old man cleared his throat, preparing to continue the ceremony, when a voice emerged that was far too familiar to me.

"I object," was all he said, his tone smooth, unafraid.

Sir Gavin.

Chapter Twenty-Seven

GAVIN

I stood firm in the middle of the aisle, in full Credian armor. I watched Myla from the corner of the courtyard, dreading every step walking toward this man. It had enraged me. I almost didn't wait until she had made it down to him.

Knights swarmed around Wyatt and Myla as the realization of my objection hit the crowd. All eyes turned to me, including Wyatt's, filled with rage.

"I gave you a chance to live. You should've taken it." He waved his hand in the air. "Guards, seize him."

Myla screamed to me, "Gavin, run!"

But I unsheathed my sword and aimed it toward Prince Wyatt. "I challenge you, here and now, for her hand." Wyatt held up his hand to the fellow knights in the courtyard, making them halt as they surrounded me.

"Is this some kind of joke to you, Sir Gavin?" Wyatt hissed between clenched teeth.

"No, are you scared you'll lose to a lowly knight, Your Highness?" I layered my words with smooth confidence. Myla looked at me, her eyes wide with fear as she shook her head. I noticed she was thinner, less like herself, and it angered me further. "We all know you're too haughty to turn down a challenge," I said, clenching my fist tighter around my sword. Wyatt laughed a hollow, evil laugh to himself before he continued.

"What is it with you and my bride, knight? Why did you come back here?"

"Because I love her." I peered at Myla when I said it aloud for the first time for the world to hear. A single tear slipped down her face. The crowd gasped at my words. "And she loves me, even when all I offered her was myself." Wyatt scoffed, making his face go cold.

"When I win, you die, but I have to give you credit for bravery, Sir Gavin." His eyes darkened as he pulled out the sword sheathed at his side. "Protect my bride," he commanded, and four knights surrounded Myla, rooting her where she stood.

Wyatt stepped forward while all the royal guests abandoned their seats. Some gathered around the courtyard, out of the way, while others gasped and squealed, taking shelter inside the castle, their footsteps echoing around the yard like a stampede. He stood there, observing me. The tension rose before he lunged forward, swinging, double handing the sword. The recoil of the blade from blocking his blow shot pain straight to my shoulders. He was angry and fighting with force rather than strategy.

His every strike was filled with his wrath.

Left, right, left, step. His swings were relentless, but I waited for the right time to make my next move, taking the time to study what he might do next until I had an opening. He brought his blade down once more, and I blocked the blow with my shoulder and jabbed my blade forward, piercing his side. The shock of pain rattled through my armor and into my bones, but Prince Wyatt fell backward, landing on his back. I stiffened my arm straight, bringing the tip of my blade down to meet his chest as his breath heaved and sweat beaded from his brow. He put all his strength into the battle with no strategic thought.

"Knights, seize him!" he snapped, holding his chin high. I never removed my sword, even as knights appeared around me with blades drawn, ready for blood. I bounced on each heel with anticipation as my eyes volleyed between the knights surrounding me.

Chapter Twenty-Eight

MYLA

The happiness I felt from seeing Gavin quickly turned to fear. Did he even think this through? Wyatt was going to kill him regardless if he won. Watching from behind the knights made my breaths burst in and out of my body, my chest pained from my racing heart, and dizziness took over from the fear coursing through me. Everything happened too quickly for me to process. Someone else pulled me out of my internal turmoil, an all too familiar voice.

"Myla," Roland whispered, dressed in Credian armor, pretending to be one of the knights protecting me. My eyes widened at the realization, but he held his finger up to where his lips would be behind his helmet and glanced over to one of the other knights a foot in front of him, his sword still sheathed at his side while they watched the fight play out between Gavin and the Prince.

I knew what he was insinuating from his smirk alone when he lifted the front of the helmet. The crowd gasped, making us look forward to watch Wyatt on the ground and see Gavin victorious. Now was our only chance. I grabbed the knight's sword in front of me and kicked his lower back, knocking him to the ground.

Everyone still paid attention to Gavin's performance. Roland took down the other two knights with ease in their distracted state. Roland gestured to the left, telling me that was the side he was taking while I went to the right. The sword felt heavy in my hands, but my muscles remembered the weight of a blade.

Prince Wyatt never took his eyes off Gavin, laughing with a heavy edge in his tone, fully believing he was about to watch Gavin's death play out before his eyes. A rush of armored bodies clashed against one another. The clang of metal and swords vibrated through the air, through the screams of the royal guests caught in between the bloodshed. I swung my sword with precision, hitting my marks with every blow.

Nobody expected a princess to know how to wield a sword. Disguised Credian knights littered the courtyard in the mix with the real ones. Gavin had brought reinforcements. Everything was perfectly planned. I made a note to thank whoever the brave strangers were as I pushed on.

Prince Wyatt ran into the castle, holding his gushing side in panic like the rich coward he was as Gavin found me amongst the chaos. His moody blue eyes met mine, and the ball of emotions sunk into my chest. I rushed forward to him as a knight came from the side, paying no attention to me as he went for Gavin. I jabbed forward, piercing him with my blade while using my foot to push him back off of it. The man fell face-first into the dirt. Gavin stepped over him, unfazed, never leaving my eyes.

He wrapped his arm around my waist, both of our faces dirty, my dress splattered with blood, the ivory white lace frayed and tattered. But nothing else mattered other than the feeling of being together again. Our lips collided, and my breath caught in my chest as I savored each slow, passionate movement of his mouth over mine.

"Guys! Another time!" Roland yelled between the swings of his sword as more knights swarmed through the castle's garden doors.

"Time to go," Gavin said, leaning his sweaty forehead against mine with a throaty rasp, still trying to catch his breath from battle and our kiss. The feel of his warmth made finches fly in the depths of my stomach that I hadn't felt in what seemed like a lifetime. Roland and Gavin picked off knights between running through the back of the courtyard. The battle divided as imposter knights ran in every direction to escape with us.

A thick rope lay over the top of the royal stone wall, which they must have placed when they snuck in to crash the wedding. Roland went first, and I followed behind him, struggling to make my way up the rope and over the wall from the last week or so with little food, and my body was already exhausted from the brief battle.

I was sure that not training since being in Credia had definitely put a damper on my progress, too. I slid down the short distance of the wall to the ground, waiting as Gavin shortly followed behind me. We ran through the woods where two horses were tied up, prepared, and ready to go.

One I certainly recognized, Max, and Gavin helped me on him before quickly slipping his leg over behind me with ease and instantly rushing Max to a gallop. The cold air chapped my cheeks, but Gavin's powerful arms wrapped on either side of me warmed something within me even against winter's chill. I looked up at him over my shoulder; the wind whistled against us as we soared forward.

He felt my eyes and met them, and I couldn't help the smile that spread across my features. His face mimicked mine as he leaned down to kiss me. Nothing could damper the joy soaring through me at being reunited with my knight, the love of my life.

We ran the horses the rest of the day, well into the night, stopping for minor breaks until we had to stop and take longer than a moment to catch our breath from the constant running. At this rate, we'd be back in Gavin's hometown soon. Roland tied up the horses close to the river for water and gave them a bag of grain to share, looking me over while he did.

"What?" I asked, my brow furrowed.

"Nothing, I was just thinking about the time you ran into battle in leathers and a crown." He grinned, looking me over once more. "And now you look like a wedding warrior in a bloody dress with a tiara." He laughed.

"The tiara really adds a special flare," I joked, and we both laughed. My first genuine laugh since before the goons took me to Prince Wyatt. Gavin walked up behind me, wrapping his arms around my waist, and I leaned back against his solid frame, lifting my arm to cup the back of his warm neck. He tucked his head into the crook of my shoulder, taking in a deep, sighing breath.

"Thank you." I looked to Roland and Gavin tightened his grip around me. "To both of you, to everyone, for saving me." Gavin turned me around to face him, his grip around my waist unwavering.

"I'll always fight for you—" I cut off his words with my own.

"I love you." My eyes lined with tears at the feelings I had for this man bursting in my chest. I was thrilled I finally was able to tell him how much he meant to me. My heart overflowing,

I wanted to say it again and again. "I—" But his lips crashed against mine, cutting off my words as he pulled my face to his.

His thumbs swept across my chapped cheeks, and heat flushed my face as he tangled his fists in my hair at the nape of my neck, deepening our kiss. His lips were soft and slow, filled with a gentleness but strong, with a need for more. Heat pooled in my center, and tingles skated down my spine.

"Ahem," sounded from a few feet away, and we both pulled back, smiling at Roland leaning up against a nearby tree and enjoying the show.

"Could you guys—" But Roland's voice stopped as he cocked his head to the side and held up a finger to us as if he were listening for something in the silence. The thunder rumbled the soil we were standing on. Roland and Gavin quickly realized that it wasn't thunder, it was the galloping hooves of horses pounding against the earth.

Gavin rushed to Max's side, grabbed my hips, and practically threw me on top. Being on top of Max again sent aches down my legs and into my hips from the long day's ride already, but we were almost there. Once again, Gavin sent Max galloping, Roland close behind us. We rode until the thundering sounds quieted in the distance behind us and continued until we could see the dimmed lantern lights shining from Gavin's hometown.

Chapter Twenty-Nine

MYLA

Beth ran out to us, looking frantic, her hair hanging in a loose bun with her shorter locks hanging free, framing her face as Gavin helped me down from Max's back. Beth took Max's reins, handing them off to Beckett to take him back to the barn. She wrapped us both into a hug.

"We don't have much time." She urged us forward hastily, our bags already waiting on the porch. A carriage sat in front of the house, readied with horses. "I packed the necessities for your journey ahead." She grabbed them with shaky hands, handing them to us with tear-filled eyes. Gavin dropped his bag and wrapped his mother in his arms, and Beth released a sob.

"I just got you back," she cried into his chest, but Gavin pulled her away to see his face.

"You did just get me back, but this time you're not losing me forever." Beth composed herself and wiped away the last of the tears in her eyes.

"The boat is down the beach. You must get going," she said, and I glanced at Gavin in question right when Roland rounded the house with Harper on his arm, and I ran to her, jumping into a hug that almost knocked us both into the dirt.

She laughed. "I've missed you too! I wish we had more time, but that'll have to wait," she said with glossy eyes.

"You're engaged!" I squealed, and she laughed again.

"That's what you're worried about?"

"I'm so happy for you, for both of you," I said, pulling her into another hug. She pulled back, wiping away her tears.

"We will write letters all the time. We can come up with our own secret code and everything."

I smiled at her excitement but asked, "where will you be?" I glanced around at Beth and the others. "Where will all of you go?"

"Beth and Gavin planned for them to leave to his father's old hunting cabin the night of the potluck so they'd be safe from your father if he came for them." I glanced at Beth, realizing that when they had walked into the house together in conversation, Gavin had already been planning to run with me. She gave me a warm smile that brought the sting of tears back to my eyes.

"But what about you and Roland?" I asked, squeezing her hands in mine.

"His family has welcomed me with open arms. I'm sure we'll figure something out. Besides, Beth told me we'd always be welcome." I thought back to how cheery Roland's father, Beau, was and knew Harper would fit right in with them.

"Myla." I heard my name from Gavin, and he nodded in the direction we needed to head. I pulled Harper in again one last time.

"I'll let you know as soon as we're someplace safe."

"I'll be waiting for it." I gathered myself and walked to Gavin, giving Roland, Wesley, and Beckett their last hugs until we saw them again one day. Gavin's brothers loaded into the carriage and I leaned down, kneeling in front of Jocelyn.

"Here," I said while taking off my crown and placing it atop her head. "This is a royal crown for a princess, and I want you to have it." She beamed when I placed it on her head and tackled me into a hug.

"Thank you, Myla!" She ran off, ready to show it to her mother, Beth, who was still standing on the porch as if saying goodbye to her family home. She mouthed *thank you* to me, and I gave her another warm smile and an acknowledging nod. Gavin offered his hand to help me stand, and I took it as we peered back one last time at the people we cared about most waving their last goodbyes. Once out of sight, we rushed to the boat, running down the switchback trails to get to the beach.

"How did we get a boat?" I asked when it came into view.

"Beau gave it to us. He wanted to help and so did some of the townspeople, who dressed as knights to save you."

The thought of all the love and kindness to help us run away together made my heart stumble over itself. I looked out towards the horizon where the sun was peeking above the waterline in the distance, cascading bright pinks and faint orange glows against the soft waves. The beach was just as beautiful at daybreak as it was at nightfall. I turned toward Gavin and his eyes were already on me, full of love and compassion. He held out his hand.

"Come on, our adventure awaits." I took it, and for the first time in my life, I was completely free and felt the most loved I'd ever felt. I didn't know where this life would lead us. I knew it would be a life of adventure and hiding from those who would come for their vengeance. But as long as we had each other, we would never stop fighting.

THE END

Thank you

for reading Myla and Gavin's story!
If you enjoyed The Promised Princess please consider leaving a review, and follow along with Lashell's author journey.
Her next release is a fantasy romance series.
Prequel novellas to her up coming fantasy series will be available to her newsletter subscribers.

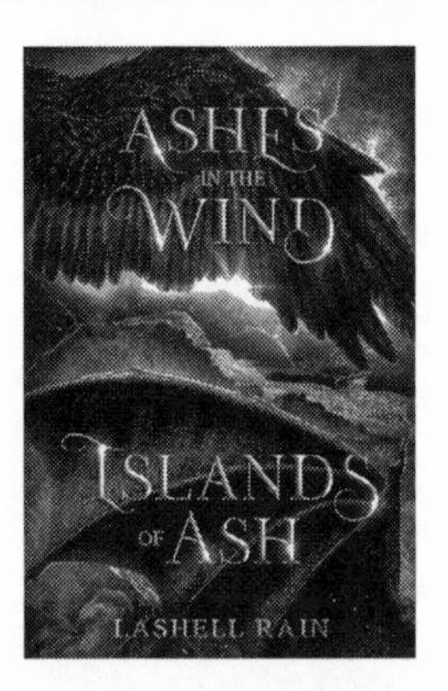

To receive updates on up coming stories, bonus content, and deleted scenes you can sign up to her newsletter from her website www.lashellrain.com

Or follow along on social media

Facebook- Author Lashell Rain

Instagram- lashell.rain.writes

Tiktok- lashell.rain.writes

Acknowledgments

First and foremost, I want to thank my husband Levi, for being a wonderful provider and father to our kids, making it possible for me to stay home and write. My stories wouldn't be possible without you busting your butt every day to hold down our family fort.

Thank you to my beautiful children for being patient with me (or at least trying to be) as I wrote this story and continue to write new adventures.

To my mom; thank you for teaching and instilling in me that if you want something in life, you can't just wish it to be, you have to work hard to get it. I wouldn't be where I am today without that advice growing up.

To my brother; if you ever read this (that's doubtful) but if you do... no you didn't. Also, what's up?! Call me sometime, and we can hang out and go to Shell Shack together!

To the amazing community of friends I've made on TikTok; Thank you, from the bottom of my heart, for your support and for welcoming me into the bookish community. Without you, I wouldn't have ever published. You all inspired me to reach for the stars and write the dang thing!

To Elise Hitchings from Reedsy; Thank you so much for your incredible editing assessment and for elevating my story to be the best it could be!

To Norma Gambini from Normas Nook Proofreading; Thank you for all of your support and amazing eagle eyes for your proofreading skills.

To Miblart; Thank you for the beautiful cover!

Special Mentions

Lylah Taylor

To Taylor; You have put up with my minor and major freakouts that come with being an author. From talking with me on the phone for hours plotting our books to being my critique partner, alpha reader, and soundboard. My books wouldn't be where they are today without your insight. Buckle up bestie, because you're stuck with me forever!

AK Mulford

To Ali; Where do I even begin? You have been one of the biggest inspirations throughout my author journey. You filled me with confidence I never would have had on my own with becoming an author. Thank you for your support and for your stories. Your characters live in my mind rent-free.

K. Elle Morrison

To Kate; You and Ali go hand in hand! But you have been the biggest help with answering all of my author questions. From helping me find beta/arc readers, to helping me set up my website. The day I bought my computer to follow my author dreams, you were the first person I wanted to tell! Thank you for all of your help and for telling me I could do it on the days I felt like I couldn't.

Stephanie Bane

To Steph; You have been my biggest fan throughout my author journey. Always cheering me on from the sidelines of our busy lives. Through it all, we always found the time to zoom for writing sprints or stay up way too late talking about our books rather than writing them. Thank you for cheering me on and being my soundboard when I needed it.

Catrina Burgess

To Cat; Thank you for all your morning ramblings filled with your two cents and telling it like it is! You were the one who pulled me through the mid-book quicksand of imposter syndrome and gave me the pull I needed to keep going. I can't thank you enough for all your tough love. It kept me motivated to keep moving forward to accomplish my dreams of becoming an author.

Eva Moore

To Eva; Thank you so much for the late-night writers club! I wouldn't get nearly as much done without it. Your words of encouragement gave me the motivation to keep going when I felt like I wanted to throw in the towel. And to all my author friends in the club, thank you so much for all your support, from being beta readers to arc readers, the love and support the club shares for one another is another huge motivation to never give up. As Eva would say, good words, everyone!

About The Author

Lashell Rain is a foodie fueled by a shameless amount of caffeine and a passion for storytelling. The Texas native lives at home with her two beautiful kids. Between being a mom by day, and a writer by night, she brought her dreams of becoming an author into a reality—by flying by the seat of her pants.

Made in the USA
Las Vegas, NV
12 September 2022